FINDING
FORRESTER

FINDING FORRESTER

A Novel by James W. Ellison,
Based on the Screenplay Written by Mike Rich

Newmarket Press • New York

First Newmarket Edition December 2000

10 9 8 7 6 5 4 3 2 1

ISBN 1-55704-479-1

Quantity Purchases

Companies, professional groups, clubs, and other organizations may qualify for special terms when ordering quantities of this title. For information, write to Special Sales, Newmarket Press, 18 East 48th Street, New York, NY 10017, call (212) 832-3575 or (800) 669-3903; FAX (212) 832-3629; or E-mail sales@newmarketpress.com
Website www.newmarketpress.com

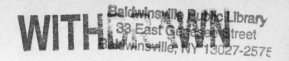

PART ONE

Chapter 1

"Jamal . . . ?"

Silence.

Janice Wallace moved a step closer to her son's bedroom door, and unconsciously her hands moved to her hips and she tapped a foot impatiently.

"Jamal?"

Silence.

On the other side of the door, sixteen-year-old Jamal Wallace opened one eye, stared unseeingly at the ceiling, then closed it and released a shuddering sigh from deep within.

"Jamal, come on now, it's seven-fifteen. You want me to come busting in there?"

"Ma—I'm up."

Jamal's eyes remained closed, but he began stretching his body and wiggling various limbs, as though testing to see if he still had possession of all his body parts.

"I wrote everything down for you," Mrs. Wallace said. "It's on the kitchen table. I've got that meeting with your teacher this afternoon and then I've got to go back to work. They need me late today, so you're gonna have to take care of yourself for dinner. Okay, baby?"

Silence.

"Jamal Wallace, I'm talking to you, boy."

"Yes, Ma."

"*Okay?*"

"Don't worry. I'll fix myself something."

"You really up now?"

"Ma, I'm *up*."

Mrs. Wallace smiled fondly at the door and shook her head. Her son never ceased to amaze her. Where had the boy come from and how was it that he had happened to grow inside of her? He was gifted at studies, and he excelled at sports, and was a good son who gave her no real trouble. She sometimes thought of his mind as a restless animal that never stopped prowling and exploring. Yes, he was a typical teenager in so many ways—he was a procrastinator, a messy eater who never sat straight at the table and shoveled his food in with his face inches from the plate, and sometimes he was locked in moods where she couldn't reach him. But his teen ways were a minor part of Jamal. He questioned everything; he took nothing on faith—and most of the time he was kind and gentle with her, and helpful around the house. God knows, it wasn't easy bringing up a young male in the South Bronx without a father—especially a young black male. Mrs. Wallace crossed her fingers and her frown turned to a smile. *God is watching me with this boy. God is watching us both.*

When Jamal heard the key give a death rattle in the lock, he rose slowly to a sitting position and squinted at the alarm clock beside his bed: seven twenty-six. He had meant to get up at seven this morning but had forgotten to set the alarm. His mother was always on his case—remember this, remember that. She told him he was such a brilliant boy with books and ideas and yet lacked the common sense to put on socks that matched, or set his alarm clock, or remember to take the lunch money she left for him each morning.

It's true, Jamal admitted to himself as he hung his long, spindly legs over the side of the bed and gave a huge yawn. *I'm kind of absentminded, like an old man who's losing his marbles.*

His bedroom, if you looked at the right wall, was the room of an ordinary sixteen-year-old boy, but Jamal was far from ordinary. His room was very small—no more than eleven-by-eleven square feet—but he considered it his citadel, his sanctuary. Nobody was allowed in it—not even his older brother Terrell, not his mother, not his friends in the neighborhood. No one, no time. He had made a pact with his mother that he would clean it himself. Every Saturday he vacuumed the floor, changed the bedsheets and washed the single small window that looked out on his piece of the South Bronx—a world of abandoned buildings and urban decay.

As he sat there coming awake, he studied the wall opposite his bed. That was the wall that would tell you, if you were allowed a look, that Jamal Wallace was no ordinary boy. He had piled milk crates to the ceiling—discarded crates from the Key Supermarket two blocks away—and they were overflowing with books: old dog-eared books he'd picked up for a song from the bargain trays at the Strand Bookstore in Manhattan. Hundreds of paperbacks, most of their names legendary to literature—Hemingway, Fitzgerald, Faulkner, Steinbeck. And the European and English novelists—Mann, Kafka, Camus, Balzac, Zola, Dickens, Maugham, Austen. And the great thinkers, from Socrates to Sartre. They were all there, Jamal's loyal mentors and friends, his lifeline to the world of ideas. He had not read every title lined up neatly in those crates, but he was coming close. Whenever he awoke in the night, there would be a book by his side. He would read until his eyes grew heavy, sometimes straight through till morning. He read voraciously, the way a starving man eats. There were thousands of questions flooding his mind, and those books were his way of reaching out for answers.

Jamal's glance moved to the wall facing the street, the wall of an ordinary teenager. A small smile creased his thin cheeks. Represented there was his other life. The public Jamal—the boy others saw and thought they knew. Basketball and baseball posters were plastered on the wall. A New York Knicks jersey served as a shade for his window. A basketball trophy he had won as a high school freshman was mounted on a sheet of beaver board and nailed to his wall.

Jamal dressed quickly, spread a blanket over his twisted sheets, his special bed-making system, and brushed his teeth. While running a pick absently through his short hair, he shambled into the kitchen and drank a large glass of orange juice as he stood at the refrigerator. He then grabbed his backpack and, for the second time that week, left the apartment without his lunch money.

Outside, he took a deep breath and exhaled. He slouched along toward school, his hands stuffed deep in his pockets, head and shoulders bent forward from the weight of his backpack. He hummed as he walked. Jamal often hummed when he anticipated something pleasant, and he was meeting his friends this morning for a pickup game before school. Jamal loved basketball—the flow, the teamwork, the testing of skills. He possessed grace and speed and a great natural shooting touch, and at six feet he could outjump many players four to six inches taller.

The game was already in progress. Jamal dropped his backpack on a bench and bent over, carefully lacing his sneakers extra tight, with a double bow. He then pulled his tube socks up as high as they would go, a pre-game ritual he did without thinking.

As he watched, his best buddy, Fly Black, faked his way by a player futilely trying to front him and soared up for a powerful dunk, rattling the chain-link netting. He turned to the player he had aced out and said, grinning, "Twelve to eight, baby, the good guys on top. Chains are singin' this morning." He motioned for the ball back. The other player bounced it to him, hard, and said, "Game ain't over, man."

"You gonna wish it was," Fly said, with a deep chuckle. At sixteen, Fly was six-four, well muscled and had the husky baritone voice of a thirty-year-old man.

Jamal approached the outdoor court, doing a wide sweep around the garbage cans, which were overloaded, ripe, and had no lids. A swarm of flies created a cloud above them.

Jesus, what a dump we live in, he thought. This is the life that surrounds us every day and tries to suck us in—high on crime, low on dreams.

"Jamal, my man," Fly said, doing a chest bump and a three-part shake. "Where you been? Gonna have to dock your pay."

"Slept late," Jamal said, grinning. "Was up late thinkin' 'bout how I was gonna save you out here." He took the ball Fly tossed him and, seemingly without looking at the basket, drained a shot.

"Gonna have to remove your privileges," Fly said.

"Ain't got no privileges."

"The ones you ain't got, they go, too."

Jamal walked out onto the court, a slab of broken concrete with grass growing in the cracks. His tread was suddenly lighter, the slouching movements gone. His adrenaline was beginning to pump his blood; his eyes were bright now, no longer sleepy. Game time!

"Hey, wait up here, man," the tallest player on the opposing team said to Fly. "You already got your team. You don't be adding no players now."

"Substitute, man. Clay, take a rest now." Clay Tully, one of the shorter players, carrying some baby fat around the middle, pushed out his mouth in a pout as Jamal replaced him.

"We got it now, Jamal, my man. We got our ducks lined up in a row." He tossed the ball to Jamal and started sprinting downcourt, yelling, "Let's shoot 'em down, man. Bust 'em up."

With Jamal in, the game slid into a higher gear. Thoroughly awake now, intensity glowing in his dark brown eyes, he slashed to the rim, leaving the kid guarding him stumbling and flailing for position. Jamal's talent, though still raw, particularly in the finer nuances of defense, was a cut above the other players,

11

including Fly. There was little swagger to his game, but a lot of quiet confidence. He knew he was good, and he let his game speak for itself; it wasn't in his nature to play himself up too much. Still, like all the others he loved to bait and bad-mouth the opposing players.

Fly taunted the kid Jamal had faked out, saying, "He sure broke your ankles good, man."

Fly quickly tossed the ball to a teammate, who, while in the air, found Jamal with a perfectly angled bounce pass. Jamal dribbled from one hand to the other, tempting the kid guarding him, leaning close, then dribbling away, sneakers squeaking on asphalt.

"C'mon," Jamal said to the kid, who again was stumbling in an effort to stay with him. "C'mon—you got somethin' to show me or not?" Baited, the kid lunged for the ball. Jamal shoulder faked him and swished from the outside. All net. "Guess you got nothin', boy," he said, but it was a good-natured taunt, no gloating or intention to hurt.

Fly held the ball on the sidelines, ready to throw it in, but then stopped as he noticed a black BMW, gleaming, perfectly polished, pull to a stop at the curb across the street. The other players stopped to stare. A car like this was dramatically out of place in their neighborhood.

"Belongs on Sutton Place," Jamal said, echoing in his own way the thoughts of all of them.

Fly punched his friend on the arm and said, "What's this about Sutton Place, bro? What you know about Sutton Place?"

"Nothin'," Jamal said, a little defensively. "It's just a ritzy part of Manhattan, is all."

As they watched, the driver of the BMW got out and smoothed down the crease of his trousers. He looked up and down the street as though he expected to see something he was not sure he was going to like. He was in his late twenties, well groomed—and white. White in a part of the Bronx where you could go an entire day and not see a single white face.

"Guess he be Sutton Place, too," Fly said, giving Jamal a hard nudge in the ribs.

"Well, he sure do go well with the car."

The well-dressed white man set the car alarm with one hand, while holding a brown grocery bag with the other.

Clay, laughing and pointing, twirled the ball on his finger, and said, "Lotta good that's gonna do. Can dismantle that in a heartbeat."

Fly said, "He's bringin' something' for the guy in the window."

The young man, carrying the bag protectively against his jacket, was still glancing around nervously as he entered the old apartment building, which was directly across the street from the schoolyard.

Clay said to Fly, "You ever seen the dude that lives up there?"

"Naw—just like, you know, shadows moving around. He stands in the window. But I know one thing—he sees us."

"Sometimes he doesn't move for minutes," Jamal said.

"Yeah, he's watching us out that window," Fly said. "I can almost feel his eyes."

Damon, a powerfully built boy with slow movements and a slow, sly manner, a member of Jamal's crew, said, "Maybe he got bodies buried up there. Cuts 'em up, drains the blood, wraps 'em in garbage bags and puts 'em under the floor slats."

"You've seen one too many horror flicks, man," Jamal said.

The cluster of young players looked up at the picture window on the second floor. That particular window was sparkling clean, unlike the dirty and cracked windows that surrounded it. Its very cleanliness only added to the mystery.

The players returned to their game, only minutes before the school bell rang. Jamal scored two quick buckets, putting the

13

game away, Fly yelling, "Take 'em down, man—take 'em *down*."

As the game ended and the players drifted off, with reluctance, for the start of the school day, Jamal lingered for a moment, slowly re-lacing his sneakers. He stared up at the window. Now he could see a figure hidden in the shadows through a gap in the curtains. Jamal continued to stare, holding his breath. At that moment the sun caught something that glittered—a pair of golden eyes winking brilliantly down at Jamal. Then the glitter was gone as the sun ducked under a cloud.

Binoculars. Whoever was in the window was watching them through binoculars. Jamal felt a chill of apprehension as he strapped on his backpack and moved off for school. For some reason, he didn't tell his friends about the binoculars. He had planned to, but then decided to keep it to himself. It was his secret.

Chapter 2

Morning classes had dragged on and on, but finally Jamal and Fly had formed their customary clique with Damon and Kenzo.

The four friends were working on their lunches in the school cafeteria. The room was overflowing with students and to accommodate them all, the school had converted the stage, which hadn't seen a performance in years, into extra eating space. The ratty, soiled stage curtain was still in place, pulled to one side. Jamal and his friends usually sat at the far end of the stage because it provided at least a few feet of isolation from other students.

"You telling me your dad saw someone in that window one time?" Fly said.

"Yeah, true story, man. Like twenty years ago."

"I'm not believin' this," Damon said.

Fly grinned and shook his head. "Me neither."

"What? You're not believin' my old man seen someone in the window?" Kenzo scowled at Damon, who he could stand up to more easily than Fly.

"I'm not believin' you have a dad."

Kenzo took a bite of his sandwich with one hand and shook his fist at Damon with the other

"Where'd he see him, Kenzo?" Jamal asked.

"Inside."

"Inside?" Fly said. "No way he went inside, man. That's pure shuck. Like whoever's in there would kill you if you went inside."

"He had some different guy bringin' him his stuff. So my dad, he hung back, you know what I'm saying? Then he walked up and saw him." Kenzo took a huge bite of his ham and cheese sandwich and chewed as he went on with his story. "My old man said he looked like a ghost, hair goin' every which way, like that guy they got pictures of in those science books."

"Einstein," Jamal said.

"Yeah, like that."

"Was he white?" Damon said.

"You ever seen a ghost that wasn't white?" Jamal said with a grin.

"He's killed people," Damon said. "He's an axe murderer or something, you know what I mean? That's why he stays inside."

"Got to do a lot more than that to have to hide around here," Fly said.

They all laughed, recognizing there was some truth in that, but Kenzo's tone turned serious as his urban version of the ancient campfire tales began to unfold. "The window's bad news." He shook his head and his mouth tightened. "Bad news. My old man may have gone in the hall, but he never got close to the door."

"Yeah? Why not?" Jamal said.

"You don't want to know, man. People used to live on that floor. Way back in olden times. They been gone for years." He turned to Fly. "You say you gotta do a lot of bad things to have to hide in our neighborhood? I hear stuff about that guy in the window—it makes you wish it was just one person. There's these sounds in the middle of the night, people goin' in and not comin' back out. That kinda stuff." Kenzo stuffed the remainder of his sandwich in his mouth, chewed briefly, then continued. "Those people who used to live there, they left. All of 'em. They abandoned their places—and why?"

"Because the building is such a dump," Fly said.

"No, no, that ain't it. It's because they *knew,* man. He's been up there since before my old man was born. And the rule back then was, you stayed away. You didn't go near that window. Those were the rules back then—and those are still the rules, man. Stay away."

There was an uncomfortable pause, finally broken by Jamal. "Well," he said, with a straight face, "I think I'm finished with my assignment on why Kenzo is totally full of bunk."

Kenzo brushed his words away with a hand and said, "You sayin' you'd go up there?"

"He's an old man lookin' out a window," Jamal said. "That's all he's ever been. The rest is gossip to put a scare in ourselves."

Kenzo stared at Jamal and said finally, "Well, I dare you to go up there and knock on his door. We'll see how brave you are."

"Hey, good idea, man," said Damon with a grin.

"He ain't got the guts," said Kenzo.

"You know something, Kenzo? I just might take you up on that."

It was late afternoon now with dusk drawing in over the only home Jamal had ever known, a place he had named the "war zone." He was alone, standing on the cracked concrete practicing free throws. Shot after shot rained down pure. He loved the sound the ball made as it went through clean. Sixty, sixty-one, sixty-two, sixty-three. His goal was to make one hundred without a miss, then he would allow himself to head for home. If he missed, though, he would have to start all over again. Those were Jamal's rules—self-imposed, true, but they might as well have come from on high. Jamal would never think of breaking them, or letting himself off easy. Once he paused between shots and glanced at the window. Inside the apartment a dim light cast a glowing circle on the curtain, but there was no movement within. Jamal bounced the ball once, twice, three times, summoning his concentration and managing to forget the window. Seventy, seventy-one, seventy-two. Clean swishes. Beautiful. I've got the groove, he told himself with a surge of well-being.

He had no way of knowing that his mother was watching him from the window of a second-floor classroom. While she studied her son, Jamal's homeroom teacher, Ms. Joyce, was shuffling through some papers at a nearby file cabinet. At twenty-three, this was her first job in the New York public school system, and she veered daily between being terrified of her students and equally terrified that she had nothing to offer them—a sheltered Jewish girl from North Jersey. Jamal Wallace, however, was the one bright spot in her teaching world and had been from the moment that first day when he slouched into her classroom, sat in the first row directly in front of her and gave her one of the most beautiful smiles she had ever seen. From that first moment she had known he was special.

She looked up and said to Mrs. Wallace, "He still there?"

"Hmm. I'm waiting for him to miss. He never misses."

Ms. Joyce pulled out a stack of papers and joined Jamal's mother by the window.

"He's out there every afternoon, soon as school's out," Ms. Joyce said. Seeing Mrs. Wallace's concerned expression, she was quick to add, "No, please, don't worry. He's fine. He's a boy who needs physical outlets—that brain of his is buzzing all the time." She turned from the window. "Come sit with me by the desk. I want to go over some things with you."

Mrs. Wallace sat stiffly and said, "Is my son in any trouble?"

Ms. Joyce smiled. "No, not at all. He's a fine young man."

"Thank you. I've always thought so."

"Mrs. Wallace, we got his test scores back this week."

Again, Mrs. Wallace looked apprehensive; her forehead knitted in a frown. She always seemed to be steeling herself for bad news. "His tests?"

"Yes, the ones the state has us take." The teacher studied it with a slight smile and then looked up. "He didn't tell you, did he?"

Mrs. Wallace shook her head, waiting for the axe to fall. Surely there had to be an axe somewhere. She had grown used to bad news in her life. Her forty-five years had not been easy, and her history told her that such good luck as having a son like Jamal would somehow have to be paid back in some form of heartbreak.

"No, he didn't say anything, Ms. Joyce."

"Mrs. Wallace, Jamal maintains about a 'C' average here, which means he does just about enough to get by. Perhaps more significantly, it means he does just enough not to stand out."

Ms. Joyce waited for a response, but Jamal's mother was determined to say nothing more until she understood the purpose of the meeting.

"What makes Jamal's case unusual," Ms. Joyce continued, "are his test results." She held a printout in front of her, smiled and sighed. "Most kids here at Richmond don't score particularly well on their SAT's. As far as I know, until now we've never had a child score above fourteen hundred."

"And what did Jamal do?" Mrs. Wallace asked so quietly that Joyce had to lean forward to hear her.

"Your son scored fourteen fifty. And on the verbal and written, he scored a perfect eight hundred."

"My goodness, that's high, isn't it? I don't know what to say. I always knew my son was intelligent."

"He's more than that, Mrs. Wallace. Testing is not the be-all and end-all, but in these terms he's gone where few have gone before. Tests don't make you a genius, but the capacity is there."

"Why are you telling me this, Ms. Joyce? Why am I here?"

"Mrs. Wallace, kids sometimes win the gene pool lottery—I mean big time, like Jamal. You just don't hear much about it

19

when it happens here. And the worst of it is, with the number of kids we have here at Franklin, he gets lost in the shuffle with everyone else."

Mrs. Wallace struggled with herself and then decided to say what was on her mind. "My son has a firm rule. He's had it since he was thirteen, maybe even earlier. No one's allowed in his room—not even me. He keeps it clean, at least he says he does, and I've tried to honor that arrangement. But once in a while I've taken a peek inside—a mother's curiosity, I guess you could say. And, Ms. Joyce, that room is just crammed with books. From floor to ceiling. Books of every kind. And when he isn't reading in there, he's writing. He's filled dozens and dozens of notebooks with his tiny scrawl. I mean, it's so hard to read, but I guess he can read it. This all started—well, his father left us when he was eleven. He never talks about that. I once asked him if he was writing anything, and if he was if I might could read it. It was a mistake. His eyes went flat. He wouldn't talk about it. All he talks about is . . . *that*. That game." She waved toward the window and the court below.

"He's still a kid, Mrs. Wallace, and that's where he gets acceptance. Kids here don't care about what he can put on paper."

Mrs. Wallace held tight to her purse on her lap. Tension deepened the lines in her face. "Do you know what I think?"

"I'd be interested to know what you think. Your son is worth all the thought we can give him."

"Okay, I have a gifted child. I guess I've always known that. And I feel like I've failed him for not being half as intelligent as he is."

"Mrs. Wallace, the world is littered with brilliant failures." Ms. Joyce rose from her chair, walked to the window and looked down at the court. Jamal was sitting on the bench, strapping on his backpack. Mrs. Wallace joined her at the window. She smiled. "I guess he did his hundred shots."

"His what?"

"A hundred straight baskets without missing. He never leaves practice till he does that."

Ms. Joyce touched the sleeve of Mrs. Wallace's dress and said, "Your son doesn't need you to be his peer or an intellectual soul mate. He just needs you to be his mom."

Chapter 3

Jamal loved his older brother Terrell for many reasons that he was too shy to express. School had been a struggle for Terrell. He had dropped out in the eleventh grade and taken a series of odd jobs. Unlike most of his friends, though, Terrell had managed to stay out of trouble and drug free. When he worked he gave his mother one-third of every paycheck to help defray household expenses. Five years older than Jamal, he had patiently taught his little brother all the playground moves he knew, and he felt nothing but pride as he watched Jamal's talent blossom. By the time Jamal was fifteen, he could beat his brother with some frequency in games of horse and one-on-one. It was about then, too, that Jamal signed out of the library a G.E.D. instruction book and convinced Terrell that he should study for his high school equivalency diploma. Terrell showed no interest at first. But Jamal kept after him until he agreed to sit with the book for an hour each night and begin to absorb knowledge that had floated over and around him in the classroom. He passed the G.E.D. just before his twenty-first birthday, with Jamal's help. To celebrate, he bought a huge, rich chocolate cake and ate the whole thing with his little brother, who nearly got sick. Terrell laughed and said, "Now I've taught you somethin', Jamal. Know your limits. A little goes a long way."

Terrell had worked at many jobs since leaving school, and his latest was working as a ticket clerk at Yankee Stadium. He loved being connected with his beloved Yankees, and one of the perks was getting to know the players. A couple of times he'd gone out with Derek Jeter for beers after a night game.

Jamal rode his bike to the stadium one evening. It was an hour before game time and a long line waited at Terrell's booth to buy tickets. Jamal locked his bike on the gatepost and knocked on the side window of his brother's booth. Terrell waved him in.

"You got some serious lines workin' tonight," Jamal said.

"The Red Sox. Always a big rivalry, Jamal. And it's the Jeter versus Garciaparra deal goin' too."

"So anything good left?"

"I got nothin' down low, little brother."

Jamal squeezed into the booth, shrugging off his backpack. "C'mon, man, not *one?*"

"Not with Boston. We're gonna sell every seat in the house. I got 'C' level, right field, ten up. It's waitin' for you. You want it?"

"Beggars can't be choosers." Jamal hopped up on the cluttered back counter and reached for the ticket Terrell had already taped to the side glass.

"Mom called tonight about those tests you took." Terrell paused to make change and shove two tickets through the opening. "What's up with that?"

"Nothin'."

"This gonna get in the way of your plan?"

"Hey, it was your plan first, man." Jamal tried to hide his unease with a wide grin.

"Sorry, nothin' left 'cept the bleachers," Terrell informed a customer. Then to Jamal: "Yeah—I figured a year of college ball. I mean with my G.E.D. and all, some college would take a chance on me if I showed enough game. Then, you know, make the jump to the pros and start writin' checks, solvin' everyone's problems." He studied Jamal with a tight smile, but the smile did not reach his eyes. "So what happened? Here I am, sellin' tickets for a couple bucks over minimum, catch a house-painting job here and there. That's it." He stared hard at Jamal. "Guess that makes it *our* plan now, right?"

23

"Yeah, right. Look, don't say anything about the tests to Fly or the other guys—okay?"

The two brothers shared an understanding glance.

"You're gonna keep that light under a barrel, little brother, aren't you?"

"Thanks for the ticket," Jamal said. "Later, man."

"Yeah, later," Terrell said. "Peace."

"Peace."

The following evening, around eleven o'clock, Jamal and Fly finished a strenuous hour of one-on-one. Except for the two boys the basketball court was deserted. They had played in semi-darkness, the only light filtering in weakly from a single streetlight on the block. They stood now at the corner of the building, staring up at the second floor.

"Check out the small corner window," Fly said. "He keeps that one cracked sometimes. One time, walkin' along on the side of the street, I thought I heard music. Like some classical stuff."

They continued to stare up at the window as they talked. Jamal checked his watch. "They're late."

A moment later, Kenzo and Damon cut through the playground. Damon signaled them with a soft low whistle.

"Were you guys here all the time?" Fly asked.

"Sittin' on the bench down the block," Damon said. "Dude could never spot us. Black on black, man."

"His lights been out for two hours," Kenzo said.

"Okay, Mister Brave Man, time to shake and bake," said Damon.

Jamal shrugged, showing no expression.

"You sure he's asleep?" Fly said.

"Guess you got to check your crystal ball to know that," Jamal said, grinning.

"Hey, that old crock must be a hundred years old," said Damon. "Sleep is what those guys do, man."

"So, we ready?" Fly said. He looked at Jamal.

"Yeah, man. Ready as I'm gonna be."

Kenzo gave a deep sigh and shook his head. "You know— maybe this isn't the best idea we ever had." He turned to Jamal. "Guy may be a homicidal maniac."

"Oh, no, man. No backin' away now. I'm down for this." Jamal started to pull his backpack off. "I'm takin' the call."

Kenzo continued shaking his head. "I always thought you was smart, man."

Fly reached for Jamal's backpack, holding it in place. "Keep it on, man. Grab a picture or somethin', so we know what he looks like."

Jamal nodded and slid his backpack higher on his shoulder.

"Okay, man," said Damon. "You need us, you drop down. We got you covered."

"Cool."

Damon and Kenzo moved off to keep watch, while Jamal and Fly crept closer to the building.

"You ready?" Fly whispered.

"Yeah, man."

"You sure?"

Jamal grinned. "Not really, man."

"Okay—up we go." Fly held his hands together, fingers laced, to give his friend a boost. Straining, he managed to lift Jamal's one hundred sixty pounds high enough so that he could grab the shallow ledge that circled the apartment. Slowly, carefully, he pulled himself up and wedged a knee onto the ledge, his athleticism helping him strike a precarious balance. He nodded down to Fly and then inched over to the window and quietly eased it open.

"Oh, man," he said under his breath. "Am I really down for this?" For the first time he realized the full weight of his mission. His heart thundered in his chest. "You're scared, man. You're really scared."

He peered inside the window and saw nothing. He pushed the curtain open and crawled through the opening. Inside the apartment now, he was past the point of no return; the time to back out had already passed. There were no lights on in the room, only the ominous shadows cast by bars of moonlight. He stood there fighting to control his breathing, trying to sense his surroundings. The only sound was a slight rustling of the curtains he had passed through.

Jamal's eyes darted from corner to corner. There was just enough light to make out the front door. Quietly, yet quickly, he tiptoed to the door and released all six dead bolts. He slowly pulled the door open a few inches, preparing himself to light out fast if he ran into trouble. He grimaced as the door gave a loud squeak. *WD-40,* Jamal thought, repressing a nervous giggle. *Door needs WD-40.*

He moved to the center of the room, trying to calm the rush of adrenaline flooding his system—*he was actually in this strange guy's apartment*—waiting for his eyes to adjust to the darkness. The room, at first, was nothing more than shades of gray and black. He remembered that book of modern art he had signed out of the library. Ad Reinhart, that was the dude's name. The severe layers of color piled one on top of the other. The room was an Ad Reinhart painting. Jamal gave an involuntary shiver. Dude had killed himself, and Jamal could understand why.

A moment later, his eyes began to penetrate the darkness. Barely an arm's length away, running along the wall as far as he could see, were shelves packed with books. The shelves ran from the floor to the high ceiling. He could now make out a wooden ladder, the kind you saw in libraries and bookstores, used to reach the higher tier of books.

Jamal moved closer, both puzzled and intrigued. His breathing slowed, his heart slowly stopped racing. He reached out and touched the bindings, most of which were in dust jackets, in mint condition, even the older titles. "This guy's a serious collector," Jamal said under his breath, as he absorbed the names—Steinbeck, Hemingway, Twain, Pynchon, Melville, Salinger, Faulkner. Same names he had, but these were no used paperbacks picked up here and there for fifty cents or a buck. Jamal was certain these were priceless first editions.

With great care he pulled a copy of *The Grapes of Wrath* from the shelf, letting his backpack slip from his shoulder onto the floor. He opened the book, one of his all-time favorites, feeling rather than seeing the words. He silently slid the book into his pack and was reaching for another when he heard a deep mumbling sound from across the room. Panicked, Jamal dropped the book and backed away in the direction of the door. Through the darkness he could see a form rising from a chair and moving slowly toward him.

Christ, man, move. Jamal sprinted for the door and frantically raced down the hallway. He took the stairs three at a time. But when he reached the lobby, he stopped and reached for his shoulder.

"Oh, no. No way." He looked back up the stairs. His backpack. He'd left his backpack in the room.

"You're a moron, man. Moron, moron, *moron. . .*"

When he emerged on the street, panting with fear and exhaustion, Fly grabbed his shoulders and said, "What's wrong. You okay, man?"

"He's up, man."

"Get outta here."

"The mother got up out of his chair—this gigantic form— I'm not exaggerating, this ain't no Kenzo baloney. I saw this big shadow moving toward me."

"Like a horror movie," Fly said, nodding.

"Worse," Jamal said. "It was real."

They were across the street now, and Jamal stole a glance at the window. Light glowed in it now, a golden rectangle, and there was the silhouette of a figure filling the space. As Jamal watched, the man raised something to the window and swung it slowly back and forth.

"My backpack," Jamal said forlornly.

"Your *what?*"

"I left my backpack up there."

"Jesus, Jamal. You always were such a simpleton. You'd lose your head if it was detachable. But, man, how could you do that?"

Jamal shrugged. "I got caught up in things. I just forgot it."

In the playground they rendezvoused with Kenzo and Damon.

Damon was hopping from foot to foot with excitement. "C'mon, man, what happened?"

Jamal was still fighting to control his breathing, to contain the panic that threatened to overwhelm him. "The guy wasn't asleep. He was right there—in the room with me."

"Get real, man," said Kenzo. "You actually saw him?"

"Not for long, man."

Fly gave Jamal a look of disgust. "This idiot left his backpack right in the guy's livin' room."

"C'mon, man," said Damon. "How could you do a thing like that?"

"I took it off and forgot."

"We wanted for you to take somethin', not leave somethin'. The guy's gonna know who you are now."

"Hey, leave it alone, man, okay?" There was an edge of anger in Jamal's voice, and an angry Jamal was such a rare occurrence that the others backed off.

"I'm gonna split," he said after an awkward pause. "It's late. Catch you men later."

"Peace," said Fly, giving Jamal fist and forearm.

"Peace, man."

"Peace," said Damon and Kenzo.

Jamal slouched off toward home, head hung low, hands jammed deep in his pockets. He felt strangely light and insubstantial without his backpack—light and wrong.

Chapter 4

Last class of the day. Ms. Joyce's classroom was full to the point that a dozen or so students were forced to sit on the counter near the shelves in the back. Franklin High, like many schools in the urban slums, had frequent teacher turnover. Burnout happened quickly at Franklin—especially among the young and idealistic who came to schools like Franklin intent on making a difference and finding that they were cogs in a machine that had long since ceased functioning. Heartbreak soon set in for the young and idealistic, and they went elsewhere, looking to make a difference and hoping for at least a glimmering of appreciation.

Ms. Joyce was an exception. She was practical, tough and determined. Hard work meant more to her than dreams of changing the system. Schools like Franklin were going down the tubes, and would continue to go down the tubes no matter how much energy and intelligence she brought to the classroom. Her view was that even these schools deserved good people to do whatever could be done to help the kids—and by God, she would do her best to make her classroom special.

Trying to keep the attention of her students and having the usual hard time, Ms. Joyce strolled to the front of a large poster of Edgar Allan Poe.

"Can any of you identify this writer?"

Silence in the classroom; not a hand was raised. You could cut the apathy with a knife. Ms. Joyce looked pointedly at Jamal, but he gave the slightest of shrugs and looked away.

"This is Edgar Allan Poe," she said. "You were assigned two

poems by him last week. He died when he was forty. Can any of you tell me how he died?"

She looked around the room, scanning the faces. Her expression and tone were tough and all-business—in sharp contrast to the compassion she had revealed with Jamal's mother.

"Come on, class. I told you last Friday what he died of."

She continued to search the faces. This time Jamal avoided her eyes.

"Well, I'll tell you," she said in a level tone, refusing to show any disappointment. Showing feelings was a weakness in a teacher, especially at a school like Franklin where the kids feasted on your vulnerabilities. She couldn't allow herself to appear weak if she hoped to teach this class anything.

"Alcohol and cocaine killed him. He was a major addict."

A tall boy with reddish dreadlocks, his long legs sprawled in the aisle, snickered.

"Can you share the joke with us, Richard?"

"There wasn't no cocaine back then."

"Yeah? Tell that to Poe."

Jamal sat on the back counter, indifference on his face. He seemed far away.

"In eighteen forty-five," Ms. Joyce continued, "Poe wrote his most famous piece, 'The Raven,' a poem he wrote at a time when he was obsessed with death."

A student sitting next to Fly turned to him and said in a loud voice, "Ravens—like the football team."

Fly, sitting low in his chair, grinned. "Hey, there's a team obsessed with death. Always gettin' their butts kicked."

"Fly," Ms. Joyce said, "a little more listening and a little less butt kicking, okay?" She stared at him but he brushed her off with a comical roll of his eyes. "Baltimore Ravens, class. The only pro team ever named after a poem. Anyone here read it?" She paused, waiting for a reaction. "Read any part of it?"

Nothing—nothing but thick apathy. "'Once upon a midnight dreary, while I pondered weak and weary?' Anybody?"

Her eyes sought Jamal's and this time found them. "Two minutes left in class," she said, "and I'm not lettin' you people run the clock out on me." She and Jamal were locked in a gaze; his expression gave her nothing. "Jamal—how 'bout it?"

He gave her a wide-eyed, innocent look. "Naw, I never read it."

There was a tense silence as they continued to stare at each other. *No disappointment, girl. You can't show disappointment.* "Okay, I need those essays by Thursday. And that's *this* Thursday."

The bell rang and the students wasted no time clearing out, but Ms. Joyce stopped Jamal at the door.

When they were alone, she said, "You gonna tell me you never read Poe?"

"What difference does it make?"

"Just answer me."

He shrugged. "Maybe some."

"Some. Just not 'The Raven,' right? Yeah, that's the one most readers of Poe never get around to."

He studied her, and she thought she saw the slightest flicker of a grin at the corner of his mouth. "You're not supposed to be sarcastic with your students, Ms. Joyce. There must be a rule about that. Franklin has rules to cover everything. How do you expect your students to learn?"

"Now I wonder who's being sarcastic. Sit down, Jamal."

"Are you asking me?"

"No. I'm telling you. *Sit.*"

Jamal slowly lowered himself onto a chair and folded his hands on his lap, watching her warily.

Leaning against the front of her desk, Ms. Joyce said, "Let's cut right to the chase, okay?"

"Whatever you say."

"Why are you afraid to show these kids what you know?"

Jamal did not answer. He looked away, breaking the connection.

"Listen, Jamal, you know, and I know, you're goin' places most of these kids will never see or know."

"Maybe."

"No maybe about it."

Jamal flashed her an annoyed look, a rare show of emotion that made him look older than his years. "So?"

"So maybe you might think about takin' some of them along for the ride. They may not get as far as you, but they'll sure get a lot further than they could without you." She paused and searched for his eyes; he was staring at his lap. "You want to be a real friend to these kids? Show them what they *can* do, instead of letting them be satisfied with what they can't."

"You're lecturing me, Ms. Joyce."

"That's right, I am."

"I don't like it."

"Tough. It's about time you heard this particular lecture from someone. What about Fly Black?"

Jamal suddenly looked alert and watchful, as though he might bolt the room.

"Aren't you two best friends?"

"Yeah. I guess."

"Fly has potential. He's a cutup in class, but he's not unintelligent. Why don't you share some of your wealth with him?"

Jamal said nothing. His face was now a blank mask.

Ms. Joyce allowed herself a sigh (*do not show disappointment*) and nodded to the classroom window. "Court sounds empty."

"Am I excused?"

"Yes, Jamal."

He got up and headed for the door, but he paused at the doorway and looked back. Ms. Joyce was already shuffling through some papers and didn't notice until she heard his voice, deep and well modulated.

"'Take thy beak from out my heart, and take thy form from off my door. Quoth the raven. . .'" He paused, a strange, unfathomable light in his eyes, and pointed to Ms. Joyce.

". . . .Nevermore," she finished.

He showed her the textbook he was carrying. "I read the book." He turned and left the room.

She shook her head and said to herself in wonder, "But 'The Raven' isn't in that book."

Fly eased up to Jamal as he slouched away from Ms. Joyce's classroom. The exits were flooded with students hurling themselves forward, eager for the outdoors and freedom.

"What she want, man. You in trouble?"

"Wants me to listen more."

"Yeah, well next time tell her listeners don't make it outta here." He punched Jamal on the arm and winked. "Not unless they got a quick first step on the court."

Jamal stopped at his locker, while Fly walked on ahead. "Later, man," he said.

"Peace."

"Peace."

*

Jamal was in bed at eleven that night, but he tossed and turned, unable to sleep. He counted to five hundred, he tried to make his mind a blank, he remembered some of his best moves on the court, but these tried-and-true methods for inducing sleep were not working tonight. Finally, at midnight, he called Fly.

After ten rings, Fly answered. He sounded alert. He never went to bed till two or later, and yet he never seemed tired.

"Hey, what's up, man?"

"How come you weren't at the court?" Jamal said.

"Ma took me to the dental clinic. Got a bunch of freakin' cavities. What you doin' up, Jamal? It's way past your bedtime."

"Something weird, man. Listen to this. I was shootin' baskets late this afternoon, doin' my hundred, you know, and I took a look at the window. You won't believe this. There's my backpack sittin' there out on the ledge."

"That's creepy, man. Really creepy."

"It's like he's taunting me."

"He don't know which of us was in there."

"I'm not so sure, man. So anyway, I'm lookin' up at my bag, just bouncing the ball and lookin' up at it, you know, and the guy's standing there in the window—full view—staring down at me. So I just grabbed the ball and took off."

"Beyond weird, man. What you gonna do?"

"That's why I'm callin' you, man. Tryin' to figure it out."

By morning, Jamal had made up his mind. Even though he had slept fitfully, he woke up full of energy and resolve, no longer wallowing in uncertainty. A decision had been made, and he was prepared to go all the way with it. He dressed quickly, grabbed his basketball and bounced it flawlessly down each of the steps to the kitchen. Mrs. Wallace was at the stove cooking scrambled eggs and sausages. As Jamal watched his mother he dribbled he ball around behind his back, from his right hand to his left hand. She turned on the water in the sink, causing the plumbing to creak and groan. The kitchen was small, the range was ancient, the walls needed painting, but Mrs. Wallace kept the space spotless.

She turned to Jamal with a look of mild reproof. "Jamal, it's Saturday morning—my day of peace and quiet. Can you hold onto that thing, please?"

He rested the ball on his hip as he reached for a piece of toast.

"It's not buttered yet."

"I like it this way."

"If you're thinking about a shower, the hot water's takin' a few minutes."

"I wasn't thinkin' about it."

He grabbed another piece of toast and headed for the door.

"Don't you want any breakfast? It's ready."

"Ma, how many times have I told you. That stuff clogs your arteries."

"Watch your manners, young man."

"I gotta go."

"You sure are in one big hurry. You meeting friends?"

"Gotta game. Yeah."

"You find your backpack yet? You'd lose your head if it wasn't tied on."

"Yeah. I left it in one of my classrooms. It got shoved back on a shelf."

"Are you sure you don't want some breakfast?"

"No way. I'm not about to put plaque in my system."

Before his mother could get in another word, Jamal was out the door. He strolled through the relative quiet of a weekend morning, bouncing and dribbling the ball as he went. The street corner loungers were off the street, deep in wine dreams. Jamal had the street to himself.

When he got to the building, he held the ball by his side to avoid making any noise. He approached the building's front entrance and looked up. The backpack was still there. Jamal paced back and forth under the ledge, careful not to walk out where he could be seen. He studied the situation from every angle, then looked at the ball in his hands. He spoke to it, saying, "You've got a job to do now. Show me what you can do."

He spun the ball in his hands, without a single dribble, concentrating his mind, and then gently shot the ball at the pack. His aim was precise, the ball hit the side of the pack, but failed to dislodge it. He tried three more times, hitting it each time, but the pack wouldn't budge.

Jamal heard the soft purr of the BMW as it turned the corner and pulled up to the curb. He held the ball tight against his chest as he watched the car. The young Ivy League guy got out—no suit this morning but still stylishly dressed in a blue blazer and a yellow polo shirt—and stood by his car, reaching inside for his briefcase and a brown bag.

When he didn't move away from the car, Jamal suddenly understood. Here was this black kid and here was this guy's precious car. It would be crazy, it would be dangerous to leave the black kid and the car alone together. Jamal had lived with this understanding all of his life. He had seen white women clutch their purses tighter to themselves when they stood next to his mother on a bus or in a department store. He had seen fear and distrust in the eyes of white folks, who were convinced he was up to no good. He had watched white kids play up to black kids to show how cool they were. Jamal hated it. Many times in his sixteen years he had brooded on the heritage of slavery. People kept telling him that things had changed; his mother was convinced that blacks were better off than they had ever been, and she held hope that one day, even if she didn't live to see it, there would be an equal playing field for all races in America. But he wondered if that was true and he wondered if things would ever really change.

He took a step toward the Ivy League guy, who stood frozen, indecisive beside his car.

"Hey, man. I'm not gonna do anything."

"I'm sorry?" A smile flickered on and off his features like a faulty lightbulb.

"I'm not about to do anything to your car."

The guy held up his hands in a peace gesture. "Hey, I wasn't thinking that."

Jamal moved closer, watching the guy's expression. He saw wariness, maybe a touch of fear. The guy was in the black world now, a separate universe, where the rules were different and where there was no way he could feel comfortable.

"This is one of those B-dash-M things, right? The ones they make in Detroit?"

Maintaining a polite smile, the Ivy League guy said, "It's a BMW. They're made in Germany."

Jamal took another step forward, close enough that he could reach out and touch the car or the guy.

"Oh, yeah, right. Germany." He bounced the ball a few times rapidly.

"You play ball?" the guy said with a big grin.

"No," Jamal said. "So it's a BMW, huh? I shoulda known." He paused, grinning at the guy, throwing him off balance. "'Cause when that company got started, it wasn't even a car company. They were makin' these engines for planes—like sixty, seventy years ago, probably. People weren't overpaying for cars back then."

The guy looked confused, and his smile slipped just slightly. Jamal reached out a hand and touched the logo. Maybe he was imagining it, but he thought the guy flinched as though he had been touched.

"That's why the 'M' stands for motor," Jamal went on. "And there's nothin' between the 'Bavarian' and the 'Works' that means cars." He paused, as though expecting a response, but the guy said nothing. He seemed to be growing impatient; his jaw twitched. "And the pilots of these blue and white planes, with their BMW engines, they'd look out the front and see this blue and white propeller as it was goin' round and round." Jamal pointed to the logo, the blue and white circle.

The Ivy League guy no longer made a pretense of friendliness. He set the car alarm, and, as he moved away from the car, said, "Thanks for the history lesson."

"No problem, man. Didn't they teach that stuff at Princeton?"

"I went to Brown."

"That must explain it."

The guy moved purposively to the door, no backward glances, and entered the building. Jamal grinned and shook his head. *I may be black,* he thought, *but the guy trusts me a little now because I'm smart and he knows I'm smart. What a screwed-up world.*

Just then, Jamal heard a thump on the sidewalk. He wheeled around, holding the ball in front of him like a shield to fend off attackers. His backpack lay on the sidewalk. Jamal glanced up, but he saw nothing inside the open window. Still, he sensed the man's presence somewhere behind the window staring down at him.

Jamal rushed home, blowing off the Saturday morning pick-up game, and ran up the stairs to his room. He dropped the pack on the card table that served as his bedroom desk. He slowly unzipped the backpack, unsure of what he would find but sensing that it would somehow be altered. Cautiously, he reached inside.

When he saw his six notebooks, he gave a sigh of relief. They were his secret passion, his real work in the world. Two years of hard work and hard thinking had gone into those notebooks: everything he could ever hope to be was contained in them. No one had ever read a word he had written, or even laid eyes on the notebooks, and he was not sure that anyone ever would. Those notebooks were the one thing in life that belonged to him, and to him alone.

He took a deep breath and cracked open the top notebook. His eyes widened as they raced down the first page. He stopped breathing. He leafed through the notebook with feverish haste, then opened the others and scanned the contents. Notes everywhere. Notes filled the margins of every page. They were written in a tiny, precise hand, and the more Jamal studied them the more struck he was with their brilliance. The man had torn his work to shreds, and yet the care and insight that had gone into his critiques were signs to Jamal that his work had value.

Hours passed. He was oblivious to the phone, to his mother pounding on the door threatening to bust in, to his hunger and thirst. His eyes danced from one note to the next, his mouth moving as he whispered changes the man had made. By late afternoon he had worked his way through all six notebooks. He reached for a fresh notebook and began to write. He did not stop writing until late Saturday afternoon.

By that evening, he knew he could not stay away. No matter what might be in store for him, he had to see the man who had performed this incredible sleight of hand, this magic. He walked slowly to the building, clutching his notebooks. He walked up the flight of stairs to the second floor. Peering around the stair-well, he saw the empty hallway and the apartment at the far end. He approached the door and knocked. No answer. Jamal was frightened and his breath was coming in short bursts. Part of him wanted to walk back down the stairs and go home, but he knew there was no turning back. By reading his notebooks, the man had altered his world by entering it—the first person ever allowed in. This man now knew what he thought and felt, and there was no turning back from that.

Jamal knocked a second time, waited, then a third time. Still nothing. Conventional knocking was not getting it done and so Jamal raised his fist and began pounding on the door. He was not going to be denied. A moment later he heard the shuffling of feet. He held his breath, waiting. A peephole in the door slid back—the large, square, old-fashioned kind that provided two-way viewing—and was filled with the glare of a dark eye. Jamal could feel more than see the intense hostility that radiated from that single eye. The glare went on, and Jamal, holding onto his nerve for dear life, continued to stare back. *This is like basket-ball when everything's at stake,* he thought. *Talent is one thing, but sometimes it takes guts to hang in there and make the game yours.*

"Hey," he said at last. "I know you're in there." He waited. Nothing. Clearing his throat nervously, he forced himself on.

"The other night—well, it was just this dare thing we do. I didn't mean any harm. Really, it was just—okay, it was stupid."

The peephole closed. Sighing, Jamal knocked again, but there was no sound inside the apartment. "Well, I'm stubborn, too," Jamal muttered to himself. "I can stand here all night."

Just then the peephole slid open again and Jamal was confronted with the same angry stare.

Encouraged by at least this much action on the other side of the door, Jamal said, "The thing is, I was wonderin' if I could bring you some more of my notebooks, or maybe write somethin' else."

Another lengthy silence wracked Jamal's nerves. He wasn't sure if he was imagining it, but he thought the eye blinked. Then, for the first time, the man spoke. He had a deep growl of a voice—accented, maybe a trace of English or Irish, Jamal thought.

"How about five thousand words," the man said, "on why you plan to stay out of my freakin' apartment."

At which point the peephole slammed shut. Jamal knew the strange interview was over, no matter what he said or did.

On Sunday, around noon, having stayed up most of the night poring over the man's notes with one hand and writing with the other, Jamal was back at the man's door. He tried a number of gentle knocks and got no response. "C'mon, man, answer the door." He started to knock louder.

The peephole slid open and the man said, "Take your hand off my door. You want me to call the police?"

"I just"—Jamal started to stammer with nervousness—"I just came here to drop off that thing you asked me for."

"Thing? What thing?"

"You know—the five thousand words on why you want me to stay out of your place." He held out some stapled sheets of notepaper, knowing the man could see them.

41

But the eye in the peephole did not move its glare away from Jamal's face. "Here's an assignment for you. Try remembering it *exactly* as I said it." The peephole slammed shut.

Jamal stared at the door, his teeth clenching with anger. "You no-good old man."

He tossed the papers at the base of the door and stormed off.

Chapter 5

The next two days crawled by. While playing ball, Jamal would cast anxious glances at the window, hoping for some sign from the man. There was none. The man didn't even appear in the window, which was unusual. Jamal did not play with his usual energy and daring, content to pass the ball rather than shoot and not bothering to penetrate and then kick the ball out, his favorite tactic. His heart was heavy.

On Wednesday morning Jamal and his classmates, far too many classmates, crowded into Mr. Curzon's geometry class. In his late thirties and possessing a short fuse, made shorter by a three-year teaching stint at Franklin, he was trying to shout the kids into their seats.

"Okay, o*kay,* everyone. We're short on seats this morning. Sit some place and *sit now.*"

"We're short on seats every morning," Fly mumbled, loud enough for the teacher to hear.

Enrico Curzon glared at Fly. "Mr. Black, I don't want to hear your voice today unless I call on you."

Jamal, having trouble finding a seat, was working his way to the back of the room. At that moment the door opened and Ms. Joyce stuck her head inside. Smiling at Mr. Curzon, she said, "Enrico, I need Jamal Wallace for a few minutes."

Curzon hated interruptions and tried to frown, but her pretty smile softened him. Jamal turned and stared at her.

"Dr. Simon has someone here to see you."

Jamal hesitated, exchanging a quick glance with Fly.

"Okay, Jamal," said Mr. Curzon. "Your presence is required elsewhere. Get a move on."

Jamal reluctantly entered the office of Dr. Jack Simon, the principal of Franklin High. He was a stout man in his fifties, who had had a brief career as a pro football lineman before entering the educational ranks. Students dreaded being called into his office. It was often the prelude to being expelled and put out on the streets, because once you were expelled from Franklin the options were limited. Dr. Simon took infractions with the utmost seriousness. He ran a tight ship, and ran it on the sound principle of fear. Fly had named him "Warden," as in prison warden. The name had caught on.

Today, however, Dr. Simon seemed less tense than usual and had an expression on his broad face that nearly resembled a smile. Standing by his side was a preppily-dressed man Jamal had never seen before. Mrs. Wallace sat in a chair opposite Dr. Simon's desk. She twisted a handkerchief in her hands as she nervously looked up at her son with a questioning frown.

"Take a seat, Jamal," Dr. Simon said. He had never exchanged a word with Jamal before today—only the problem kids got to know Dr. Simon well—and now he was acting as though the two of them were old friends. The Warden, Jamal thought.

Jamal moved toward the empty chair next to his mother. She nodded and touched the sleeve of his shirt. "Hey, honey. . . ."

Embarrassed, he shrugged away from her hand and sat down.

Dr. Simon cleared his throat and took a sip of water from a large bottle of Poland Spring, as though he was about to embark on a speech.

"Mrs. Wallace—Jamal—this gentleman is Mr. Bradley."

The white man smiled down at Jamal. "Good to meet you, Jamal."

Jamal inclined his head forward, but said nothing.

"When we received your recent test scores," Dr. Simon continued, "we anticipated the possibility they might attract some interest from private schools. It seems we anticipated correctly." He turned stiffly in his seat. "Mr. Bradley?"

"Jamal, Mrs. Wallace," the man said in a high, patrician voice, "my name is David Bradley. I'm with the Mailor-Callow school in Manhattan. Are you familiar with it?"

Mrs. Wallace nodded. An expression crossed her face, somewhere between fear and awe.

The man trained his sky blue eyes on Jamal. "Let me tell you something about Mailor-Callow. It's not only the top preparatory school in the state, it's also regarded as the finest prep institution on the East Coast. Only the very best students go there."

Mr. Bradley paused, letting his words sink in. Jamal found the man's intent gaze unsettling and didn't know where to look. In the South Bronx you were careful about making tight eye contact with people you didn't know.

"As you might imagine," Mr. Bradley continued, "we're a few weeks into fall term, but every year we hold a few openings while we wait for the test scores to come in. Jamal—your scores, to put it mildly, caught our attention." He leaned his tall, slim body forward from the waist and said, "I'm here to see if you'd be interested in one of those openings."

Jamal glanced at his mother, but before he could respond, Dr. Simon said, "Look here, Jamal, we know that leaving for another school—especially a private one—won't be easy. But the fact is, we can't take you any further. Franklin's running thirty-five percent over capacity, and one of the main jobs I face every day is making sure the kids who come here in the morning go back home in the afternoon." He paused, searching the boy's eyes, looking for a clue to what he was thinking. But like most of kids, especially kids in the Franklin High world, he had mastered the art of showing nothing. "Son, believe me when I say, this is not a difficult choice."

Again, Jamal looked at his mother. She simply gave him a nervous, encouraging smile.

45

Finally she spoke, winding the handkerchief ever tighter around her fingers. "There's no way we can pay for any of this."

"We're not asking you to," Mr. Bradley answered gently, solemnly.

When the meeting ended, Mrs. Wallace and Jamal walked with Mr. Bradley to his car, a sparkling new Mercedes, while he continued extolling the virtues of the school. Bradley unlocked the door, reached in the glove compartment and withdrew a thick Mailor-Callow information packet. Handing it to Jamal, he said, "When Dr. Simon mentioned that only the best go to Mailor, he forgot to mention that our commitment to excellence extends beyond the classroom."

"Yeah, I know. They've won a few basketball championships. But not for a while."

Bradley nodded. "Recently we have had some lean years. But about forty of our students have gone on to play college ball, and three have made it to the professional level. We took the liberty of evaluating your play last year, and"—Bradley hesitated, gave a polite cough—"and while this is strictly an academic offer, you understand, we won't be disappointed if you choose to play."

Jamal looked at his mother, not knowing what to say. She smiled, but said nothing.

"The point is," said Bradley, pushing his pitch a little more strongly, "all we're asking is that you come visit us for a couple of days, get the feel of the place, and think it over."

He reached out and shook Jamal's hand. "Jamal, Mrs. Wallace, it's been a pleasure meeting you both."

They watched as Bradley drove off.

"So," Mrs. Wallace said, "what do you think?"

"I don't know."

"We'll talk tonight—okay?"

Jamal nodded and she straightened his coat collar.

He glanced quickly left and right to see if anyone was watching them. "Don't fuss, Ma," he said under his breath.

"You're a good kid, you know that?"

She embraced him, and he pulled quickly away.

"Mom . . . hey."

"Embarrassed by your mother?"

"Don't do that around Franklin—okay?"

"I know, I know. Go on now. I'll see you tonight."

She watched her son slouch away, pride shining in her eyes.

Jamal skipped the daily pickup game that afternoon, telling his friends he had a stomachache. At home, locked in his room, he went through his notebooks studying the revisions he had made based on the man's editing. That evening, after dinner, he walked to the man's building, climbed the stairs and stood at the door. The papers he had tossed down in anger earlier in the week were gone. Jamal smiled. For the first time he was calm standing there at the man's door; the fear was gone. He felt that he belonged now because the man, in his own unusual way, had entered his world and become a part of it.

He started to knock, but then decided he didn't want to get involved in all the baggage of the peephole, voices communicating through a door. It was a game he preferred not to play. Instead, he sat down against the wall, just next to the door, pulled a sheet of wrinkled paper from his pocket and began to write a note. "I don't know your name," he wrote, "so I can't give a proper salutation. But I have more pages for you, which I'll leave next to your door. . . ." He stopped writing when the squeaking of the peephole invaded his concentration. But he didn't stand up, or even glance at the door. He waited a moment and then said, "I didn't knock, man."

A long silence before the voice growled, "What are you doing here? Why do you persist in bothering me?"

47

"I'll tell you when I get my five thousand words back." Calmly, Jamal continued to scribble his note.

"So you do remember," the man said. Jamal heard the deadbolts creak as they were being unlocked. The door swung open and Jamal scrambled to his feet. He entered the apartment slowly. As he looked around, taking it all in in a glance, he couldn't contain his amazement. How could something like this—this elegant, this. . . *fine*—exist in his neighborhood? The living room was packed with antique, well-preserved furniture. Every wall, from floor to ceiling, was given over to shelves containing thousands of books—all hardbacks, and all as well preserved as the furniture.

As Jamal peered deeper into the room, he could see three TV sets tucked into wooden cabinets, and in that area of the apartment were glass cabinets jammed with sports memorabilia, baseball bats, Yankee and Knicks jerseys, a number of autographed baseballs and two basketballs scrawled with names. In the corner of what Jamal figured must be the living room an antique desk stood surrounded by a work area of file cabinets, small tables piled with books and manuscripts, and two typewriter tables supporting two ancient manual typewriters. The work area itself was nearly as large as Jamal's bedroom.

Plants—many varieties and all the colors of the rainbow—grew everywhere, and stationed at the man's window was a huge telescope, with two sets of binoculars draped from the telescope by black strings around their hinges.

The man, not bothering to acknowledge Jamal's presence, stood over an old cherry wood table, scrawling out thoughts on the lined paper that Jamal recognized as his own.

As he stood in the middle of the room uncertainly, Jamal studied the man. He was in his late sixties—a large bear of a man, and although his skin had the pale, fish-belly pallor of someone who lived his life indoors, he didn't look fat or soft. His white beard was carefully trimmed—like Hemingway's,

Jamal thought, remembering photographs he had seen of the great writer—and his flowing white hair was parted in the middle. His bushy eyebrows were as dark as his eyes. He had a down-turned mouth and a sorrowful, wary expression. He was dressed casually in a black turtleneck, khaki pants and a tweed jacket—like a college professor, Jamal decided, but not like any college professor he had ever imagined. There was a dangerous quality about him—dangerous and unpredictable.

When the man finally looked up, their eyes met. Something in his look told Jamal that he had advanced into the room far enough. He sensed that the man had invisible boundaries that Jamal had better honor.

The man squinted down at the papers he was holding. He said, "The man with the Mercedes this afternoon . . ." The sentence trailed off. Was it a question? Was the man keeping a close watch on him?

"He was from this private school," Jamal said. "They want me to go there."

"What school is that?" the man asked, not looking up.

"Mailor-Callow."

The man nodded without expression and kept writing.

"They're all wantin' me to do it," Jamal said, feeling he hadn't provided an adequate answer. "We don't have to pay anything, which works out, I guess. But—I don't know. I'm not sure it's for me." He paused, expecting some sort of response from the man, but he kept writing and Jamal kept talking.

"We live a few blocks from here. . . ." He waited. Nothing. "Me and my mom, I mean. My brother Terrell, my older brother, he used to live with us but he moved out about a year ago. And—and when I was eleven, that's when my dad moved out. A different kind of movin' out, though. It was around then, maybe a little later, that's when I started"—he gestured at the papers in the man's hand—"doing some of that."

"Making your own world," the man mumbled.

"What?"

"How old are you?"

"Sixteen."

"Sixteen." The man studied him for a moment. "And you're black." He shook his head. "Remarkable."

"What's me bein' black got to do with anything?" Jamal's tone was sharper than he had intended.

The man continued to study him, watching him simmer. "You don't know what to do right now, do you? If you tell me what you really want to tell me, I might not look at any more of your stuff—right? But if you let me run you down with this racist nonsense—now what does that make you?"

Jamal glared at him. "I'm not playin' that game, man."

The man handed the papers over. "I'd say you're playing it. The racist stuff is there, it stinks, you hate it, but you're still standing there. That's one game. Of course there are other games."

He turned away from Jamal, clearly dismissing him, walked to a well-stocked liquor cabinet and reached inside for a bottle of scotch.

Jamal, for one of the few times in his life at a loss for words, knew it was time to leave.

Chapter 6

When Jamal got home, Mrs. Wallace was waiting for him.

"We need to talk, honey. Terrell's here."

They sat at the kitchen table, its porcelain surface cracked and lusterless from years of wear. Mrs. Wallace tapped the Mailor-Callow brochure, printed on expensively coated paper and the size of a coffee table book. Terrell was huddled over a slice of coffee cake and a mug of steaming coffee. He grinned up at his younger brother and winked. Jamal returned the wink, but he was still back in the apartment, grappling with thoughts of the mysterious man.

"You want coffee?" his mother said.

"No."

"Can I get you anything? You don't eat enough."

"No, Ma. I'm tired. Do we have to go over this stuff tonight?"

"A family meetin', little brother," Terrell said.

Mrs. Wallace said, "Do you have any idea how much it costs to go there?"

"What difference does it make? It's free for us."

"Nothin's free in this life," said Terrell.

"Twenty-one thousand dollars, honey." Mrs. Wallace looked at Jamal, her features pinched with worry. "Do you know what that means?"

Jamal shrugged.

"It means he'll be hangin' with kids whose families can afford to pay that much," said Terrell. "Rich white kids."

Mrs. Wallace flashed a pinched, annoyed look at her older son. "Terrell, be practical for once in your life."

"I am bein' practical. Jamal can get lost in that world."

Mrs. Wallace nodded, clearly torn. "I know, I know. But how can we pass up an opportunity like this?" She turned to Jamal. "It's got to be your decision. We can't make it for you."

Jamal stared at her, but said nothing.

"What do you think? Is it somethin' you want to do?"

He reached for the brochure. "I'll take a look at it. We'll talk tomorrow."

"Just be sure you know what you're doin', little brother."

"Yeah," Jamal said.

Mrs. Wallace said, "All I know is, it's a good thing they're the ones payin' for all this."

"Let me read it, Ma." Jamal yawned, untangled his long legs from beneath the table. "I'm off to bed now. I'm beat."

"They want you to visit the school in two days. You can't be procrastinatin' on this, honey."

"Well, it doesn't do any harm to take a look, does it?" He grinned at Terrell, who regarded him seriously, not returning his smile.

*

Jamal took the 4 train into Manhattan, packed in solid, clutching a pole. He was on his way to what that guy Bradley had called the best prep school on the East Coast. Mrs. Wallace had gone shopping the day before, using money from their emergency fund, a milk bottle stuffed with bills they kept on a shelf in the kitchen. The result of her shopping was a bright striped tie, a brown and white checked shirt and brown corduroy pants on the baggy side. *A little fancy,* Jamal thought, *maybe a little flashy, too, for a place like Mailor-Callow.* He hadn't wanted to hurt his mother's feelings, but he had explained that he didn't feel comfortable wearing new clothes. After all, he was only visiting the school. He settled for his usual outfit—sneakers, jeans, and a t-shirt.

With each passing stop Jamal was moving away from his world into an unfamiliar world of whiteness and privilege. Jamal's stop was Eighty-sixth Street. Casual clothes, dark complexions and the *Daily News* had given over to suits, brief-cases, pale faces and *The New York Times*. A different world— one that neither attracted nor repelled Jamal. To become a part of it had never entered into his fantasies; he had simply assumed that it wasn't an option for kids like him.

He emerged on a busy Manhattan street, blinking in the light of a brilliant early autumn day. He weaved his way along, careful not to bump into anyone, until he spotted the dark red brick building that housed Mailor-Callow. He studied the large brass plaque at the entrance, suddenly filled with a desire to turn around and go home and forget the whole thing. What was he doing here? He didn't belong here. Students were swirling around him—he'd never seen so much blonde hair and so many blue-eyed and pink-cheeked people at one time. The girls wore expensive sweaters and skirts, the boys blue blazers and gray flannel trousers—the school's loosely enforced uni-form. Jamal knew that he looked respectable, but it was obvi-ous he was dressed for some other school, not Mailor-Callow.

Trying to hide his sudden attack of shyness and fear, he walked inside, hands in pockets, affecting a casualness he didn't feel. The hall was jammed with kids hurrying to their first classes and Jamal was an object of total indifference to them. He took a few halting steps, staring at a sheet of paper he had pulled from his shirt pocket. He was supposed to proceed to the main office. He walked along slowly, absorbing the atmosphere, the paintings on the walls (some looked familiar and he wondered if they were originals), the rich carpeting under his feet, the quiet buzzing of voices and laughter so different from the raucous craziness of a morning at Franklin High. *Could he ever get used to this?*

The moment he entered the main office, Jamal was struck more forcefully than ever by the money and power behind

Mailor-Callow. In the front of the room were four beautifully ornate wooden desks, and farther back, near the windows that looked out on the street, new computers, new fax and copy machines gleamed—new everything that wasn't antique and expensive. Jamal had never worked with anything electronic that wasn't held together by tape and wire and that functioned only when it felt like functioning. He was impressed.

He stood at the counter, but before anyone noticed him standing there, a girl walked up, smiled and said, "Are you Jamal Wallace?"

"Yeah," he answered. "Yes." He stuck out his hand stiffly. She took his in a firm grasp. Her hand was warm and dry; his was moist with anxiety.

"Claire Spence," she said. "Bradley asked me to show you around this morning."

She called Mr. Bradley by his last name. In Jamal's world that was a sign of disrespect.

"You up for a little inspection of this joint, Jamal?"

"Sure."

He finally brought himself to look directly at Claire Spence. She was around his age, maybe a year older, and she wore a white blouse and a short off-white skirt. Her hair was light brown and straight, pulled back with a barrette. Her eyes were hazel, her skin was smooth and startlingly pale. She looked expensive, Jamal thought, but nice. Not flashy.

She led him by a stride down the hallway. He was struck by the oak lockers and the pristine polished pine hallways beyond the carpeted area in the front. Jamal was in a trance; it was all a kind of dream. His eyes couldn't move fast enough to take it all in.

She turned to him and nudged his elbow with hers. Nervously, he pulled slightly away, but she didn't seem to notice. For some reason, he liked that.

She said, "Don't worry about answering any questions or anything, not till you decide what you're gonna do. Okay?"

"That's cool."

"Besides, the teachers here aren't all that much into student participation. Too busy listening to themselves talk."

Jamal slowed his pace and stared at her. "What do you mean?"

Claire opened a door that led into a massive classroom. She winked at Jamal—slowly, comically—and, grinning, said, "You'll see."

The room reminded Jamal of halls on college campuses he had read descriptions of in novels, with dozens of seats sloping down to the lecture area. He slid into a chair next to Claire near the back. He actually had enough room to stretch out his legs—a welcome novelty; at Franklin there was a scarcity of everything, including space.

Dominating the room was Professor Robert Crawford, an elderly man with a stern countenance and a precisely barbered beard. He wore a vest and a bow tie. *Wait till I tell Fly about this dude*, Jamal thought, smiling to himself. *Unreal!*

"This morning," said Crawford, clearing his throat portentously, "we begin our second required reading of the semester, the study of a novel that offers everything—and an author who could have given us much, much more."

A stack of books was handed down the row, each student taking one copy of a plain covered paperback entitled *Avalon Landing*.

Claire whispered in Jamal's ear as the books made their way back to them, "That's Robert Crawford—the *great* Robert Crawford," she added in a haughty Katharine Hepburn drawl that made Jamal laugh softly. "He's been here as long as most of the buildings."

Professor Crawford leafed through a copy, mumbling under his breath, and then peered out at the class over the top of his bifocals.

"When William Forrester was twenty-three, in nineteen fifty-three, he set out to write his first book. Many authors *talk* about writing the Great American Novel—well, William Forrester did it . . . on his first try."

Claire leaned close again and whispered, "Ever read this?"

"Yeah. You?"

"Only about a dozen times."

"Unfortunately," Crawford continued, "for whatever reasons, Forrester's first try was also his last." The professor held up the book, moving it from right to left and back again. "This was the only one he chose to publish. For all we know, it was the only one he chose to write.

"Now your job over the next week"—a moan rose from the students, which Crawford silenced with an abrupt slicing motion—"let me repeat, over the *next week,* is to read it and tell me why he stopped writing, or publishing what he wrote, in his mid-twenties."

After ten minutes of Professor Crawford, Claire and Jamal walked out the front entrance of Mailor-Callow into the bright fall sunlight.

"So what do you think of the esteemed Robert Crawford—or, if you prefer, Bob the boob?"

"Well, he kinda drones on."

"A pompous fool, is what you mean."

"I guess you could say that."

"I'm warning you, Jamal, there are a lot of teachers here like Crawford—overly fond of the sound of their own voices."

"Must be a teacher's disease. I've had my share of 'em." He suddenly thought of Ms. Joyce, and added, "But I've been lucky to get one or two good ones."

"So—you're coming back tomorrow?"

"Yeah. They want me to spend some time on the court."

"I heard."

"You heard—what? What did you hear?"

"Well, graduation last year made our already thin ranks thinner." She studied Jamal's face, her hazel eyes serious. "Hey, you okay with playing?"

"Sure. I guess."

"I mean, it's just like college, right? You get an education and they get what they want. Or maybe you both get what you want. It's playing the game."

"Maybe."

They stopped at the corner of Lexington and Eighty-sixth, ready to go their separate ways.

Claire smiled up into Jamal's eyes. "It was great meeting you."

"You gonna be around tomorrow?" he said.

"Yeah, but not where you'll be," she said in a teasing voice. "You might be able to find me for lunch, though. In fact that's tomorrow's assignment for you."

She set off down Lexington, then turned and grinned over her shoulder.

Jamal watched her walk away, his eyes bright with interest.

Chapter 7

Late that afternoon, Jamal was back at the man's apartment. He knocked once, and as he waited, he did his basketball drills—dribbling between his legs, behind his back, switching right hand to left hand and back again. He felt confident about being there, no longer apprehensive; underneath the man's gruff manner Jamal sensed his interest.

When the peephole slid open, he moved a step forward, holding the ball at his hip. "You said if I didn't say what I want to say, you might look at some more of my stuff. Well, I didn't say what I wanted to say."

The door slowly opened and Jamal entered.

"You can use the table," the man said, indicating a table next to his desk. He walked with a stiff gait back to the main window, sprayed Windex over the surface and began to clean it meticulously, not missing an edge or a corner.

Jamal watched him for a moment, then sat down. He removed a number of notebooks from his backpack and opened them. A bowl of steaming tomato soup was placed in the center of the table. The aroma was delicious, causing Jamal to swallow hungrily.

"That soup for me?"

"Apparently it is."

"Thanks, man." Jamal picked up the spoon and moved the bowl closer to him.

"Let it cool a little. It tastes better."

"Did you make this yourself? It doesn't look or smell like Campbell's."

"I abhor all canned goods."

Jamal continued to watch the man as he cleaned the window, a few inches at a time.

"I guess you were expecting me."

"Why do you say that?"

"The soup."

"Don't conjecture so much. It's there. Enjoy it."

Jamal breathed in the smell of the soup. After a moment, he said, "They talk a lot about you out there."

The only response was the squeaking sound of cloth against glass.

"Kenzo—my friend Kenzo Henderson—he does most of it. He goes on about, you know, how long you've been here, longer'n everybody, watchin' everything from that window." Jamal hesitated and then continued, saying, "And wonderin'— I guess we all have—why you've been here so long."

When the man finished cleaning the window, he began to fiddle with the telescope, making minute adjustments, clearly not accepting the invitation to reveal anything about himself.

"Man," Jamal said slowly, feeling his way along, "if it was me, I wouldn't leave—"

"Subjunctive," the man interrupted with a growl.

"What?"

"'If it *were* me.' The subjunctive. You're speculating about something that might or could be."

"I know that."

"Then why don't you say it?"

"Doesn't sound right when I say it, you know? Phony."

"Phoniness is when you're unwilling to admit what you know."

"Anyway, what I'm saying is, if it *were* me I wouldn't leave here. No way. You don't hear traffic in here, kids yelling, babies bawling all night. Our place—we've got these people who live on the other side of this paper thin bedroom wall and they've either got their kid yellin' 'cause he's only a year old, or the old man's yellin' 'cause the kid's makin' too much noise, and the only time she's yellin' is the one or two times out of the month when they're both feelin' right."

The man cut in, saying, "You need to stir that soup."

"What?"

"Stir your soup. So it doesn't firm up."

Jamal dipped his spoon in, breaking the whitish film on the surface.

"How come ours never gets anything on it?" he asked.

The man said, "Well, now. What do we have here?" He was staring intently out the window, a sudden look of curiosity brightening and softening his features. Not looking away, he reached for a video camera and held it to his eyes, focusing with his thumb and first finger. He pointed it at an object to the left of the playground across the street where there was a row of scraggly ailanthus trees.

"What we have here," he mumbled aloud, "is an adult male. Tiny yellow guy . . . ten centimeters at wing, maybe fifteen. Connecticut warbler. Standard coloring, probably a stray from the park."

When the bird flew out of his view, the man lowered the camera and glanced at Jamal, a bemused expression on his face. "A pretty bird, the Connecticut warbler. Certainly adds tone to the neighborhood."

"You ever go outside to do any of this?"

The man's features flattened again, the light going out of his eyes. "You should have stayed with the soup question." He turned and walked to his desk. With his back to Jamal, he said, "The object of a question is, or should be, what matters to us, not to anyone else." As he spoke, he opened a drawer, revealing a neat file of tiny videotapes, each with a meticulously printed bird species label. He reached for a new label, and, standing at his desk, bent over and began to write.

"You have to understand," he said, "it's like these television reporters. They ask these pathetic questions, and in the middle of the pathetic answers they get—and deserve to get—the camera cuts back so that I can see the expression of the person who *asked* the question. Now—let's assume the question *is* a decent one, which is almost never the case. What I need to see is the expression of the poor guy who's *answering* the question. You wondered why your soup doesn't firm up, which makes sense considering that your mother probably grew up in a home that never thought about wasting milk on soup when water was fine. That question was a good one"—he paused and sighed—"in contrast to 'Do I ever go outside?' which fails to meet the basic standard of obtaining information that matters to you."

Jamal was caught off guard by the man's sudden flow of words, but was not so overwhelmed that he didn't detect a possible logical flaw in the argument. "But if a really good question is important to the person askin' it—even if the question's asked by a reporter—isn't that the face you'd want to see? I mean, if the question's a really good one?"

The man shot Jamal a quick look, an eyebrow raised in surprise.

"Just tryin' to follow what you're sayin', man," Jamal added.

"Your mind's working," the man said, his gruffness slightly muted. "That's good. Most minds don't probe. Okay—let's see if I can give you a reasonable answer. Interviewers are paid to ask questions, so their questions aren't genuine in the sense that they're trying to learn something for themselves, as you were when you asked about the soup. Their questions are designed to elicit information from the interviewee, to satisfy our hunger for gossip. In a very real sense, then, they are non questions."

Jamal slowly nodded. "I don't think I have any more soup questions."

"No?"

Jamal took a sip of his soup, then looked up. The man was sitting in the chair at his desk now, holding an uncapped pen, regarding him.

Jamal put the spoon down and said, "Why'd you say those things the other day? About me bein' black?"

"It had nothing to do with your being black. It had everything to do with finding out how much nonsense you'll put up with."

"So you knew I might come back."

"Just like I know you'll decide to go to this new school."

"How do you know that?"

"Because your writing suggests a question exists as to what you wish to do with your life. And that is a question the school across the street can no longer answer for you."

Jamal was introduced to all the Mailor-Callow players by coach Peter Garrick, a red-faced intense man in his late fifties, a shouter, who seemed to pattern himself after a less fiery version of Bobby Knight. As Jamal suited up, a number of the boys came by his locker, making friendly overtures, but not John Hartwell, the only black kid on the team and the one player Jamal was hoping he might be able to rap with honestly about life at Mailor-Callow. He didn't come near Jamal, didn't introduce himself and refused to look at him when Garrick introduced him.

Within minutes of practice Jamal's jersey was soaked with sweat. They were practicing running patterns, catching passes, laying the ball in the basket. Garrick believed in maintaining a furious pace. He marched up and down the sidelines, blowing his whistle and screaming instructions and insults.

"All right," he said, his voice raspy, overworked. "Let's match up. Hartwell, I want you on Wallace. Let's wake up, team. Show me something."

"How you doin', man?" Jamal said.

Hartwell raised an eyebrow and bounced the ball in Jamal's direction, hard.

"Just check it, okay?"

"What's your problem, man?" Jamal said under his breath.

"Just check it . . . man."

Jamal slowly bounced the ball, his expression blank, giving nothing away.

"Ball's in," Hartwell called out, and he quickly pushed the ball up court, probing Jamal's defense. He was no quicker than a bunch of Jamal's classmates at Franklin, but he was better coached and his moves were slick and thoughtful—feints, deceptive eye slides, deft footwork. He faked to the left, moved right, Jamal following but a fraction behind, and hit a teammate with a precise pass for an easy lay up.

Jamal's ball now. He already knew that he had foot speed on Hartwell, but he also knew that his skills were rawer. This was going to be hard work. Hartwell backpedaled on defense, saying nothing to Jamal, but there was a look in his eyes, a cold appraising glint, which seemed to say, This is my court; you don't belong on the same court with me.

Jamal closed in on Hartwell, some of the swagger from back home entering his game. He leaned close and whispered to Hartwell, "What's it gonna be, man?" He cross dribbled, left to right, a move he had perfected, but Hartwell read it immediately and deftly stole the ball. He raced for the hoop and laid it in. Nothing fancy, Jamal noticed. No playground stuff. Nothing . . . *black.*

Hartwell gave him a tight, unpleasant grin and said, "Leave the trash back home, Wallace."

Jamal's eyes stung with anger. Running up court now, arms extended, asking for the ball, a teammate hit him with an accurate cross-court bounce pass, and he suddenly accelerated, bursting toward the hoop, covering the last few feet in the air, jamming the ball down so hard the rim rattled.

63

Coach Garrick yelled, "Hartwell—a little defense would be nice. Do your sleeping at night."

A player tossed the ball to Hartwell, who turned to find Jamal all over him like an extra suit of clothes.

"Whoa, Wallace, watch the body check."

"Get it past the line, man."

"What did you say?"

"Let's see you get it past the line. Show me what you got. Time runnin' on you, man. What you got to show me?"

Finally, in frustration, Hartwell yelled out, "Need some help!" But Jamal stopped him just short of mid court.

"Ten seconds!" Garrick yelled. "Other way."

Hartwell slammed his palms together. "Oh, man!"

The ball was thrown to Jamal, and Hartwell closed in. "C'mon, Wallace, a little more of your playground razzle dazzle."

Jamal gave a head fake again and blew by Hartwell, rising high for his shot, hitting.

Hartwell quickly got the ball back and moved up court, a wary eye on Jamal, who was close and moved in closer, hand checking Hartwell on his rib cage. Suddenly he smashed into a screen set by an opposing player and Hartwell streaked into the corner, free of Jamal. He passed to a teammate, who calmly sank a fifteen-footer.

A whistle blew the end of the game.

As Hartwell walked past Jamal he said, "That's how we do it here. In case you never heard, it's called team play."

"Lighten up, man," Jamal said, trying to curb his anger.

Hartwell grabbed a towel, mopped his face, then draped it over his shoulders. "Maybe you should consider staying where you are."

He turned away and headed for the locker room. Jamal watched him, expressionless, sweat dripping from his face onto the floor.

"Tell me about Hartwell," Jamal said to Claire. They sat at a small table in the Mailor-Callow cafeteria, barely visible beneath the trays and Claire's mound of books.

"John Hartwell's a pill," she said.

"A what?" Jamal had never heard anyone described as a pill, although he could tell from her expression it was not meant to be flattering.

"He's a rich kid who wants as much of the spotlight as he can get his senior year. That's all it is."

Jamal took a bite of his salad. The cafeteria fare at Mailor-Callow was so superior to Franklin's that he wondered if the stuff Franklin served could actually be called food. The romaine lettuce and sliced tomatoes were crisp and fresh, and the Jarlsberg cheese (Claire's suggestion; he had never tried it) was creamy and delicious.

He said between mouthfuls, "They take things pretty seriously here."

"Yeah, well—it's a serious place. Serious enough that I usually end up getting lunch on my books most days. Everybody's striving for the right college. Some of the kids here, if they don't make Harvard or Yale, their lives are over." She smiled at Jamal, then her attention drifted back to the book propped on her backpack.

"What you workin' on?"

"Forrester's novel."

"But I thought you said you'd read it. . . like—"

"Yeah, right, a dozen times. I know. My father gave me this copy." She flipped to the front and showed Jamal the title page. "See that 'A'? When this book was published, Scribner's always put an 'A' on their first editions."

"That's a real collector's item," Jamal said, impressed.

"Yeah. It was a small printing—like three, four thousand—before the publisher knew what they had. And here's the best part of all, Jamal. Look at Forrester's picture on the back. It

65

only appeared on the first edition. Once the book began to take off there was a second printing. Forrester insisted on Scribner's removing it."

Jamal stared at the photograph, his expression frozen in shock. The author was young, no more than twenty-five, and lean. He was clean-shaven and had a full head of hair—but he was unmistakably the man in the window. The man in the window was William Forrester. The man who was reading his work was the most famous American writer of his generation. He kept staring at the photograph, his thoughts a confused jumble.

Claire studied him curiously. "You okay?"

"Yeah."

"It's a great picture, isn't it? Doesn't he look so completely like a writer?"

"Yeah—he does." Jamal stood up, his lunch forgotten, the scene with Hartwell in the gym forgotten. His mind was consumed with Forrester.

"Listen," he said, "I gotta run."

"What? But we're eating lunch. What's wrong?"

"Nothing's wrong. I just forgot—there's a couple things I have to do. Catch you later."

Before Claire could respond, Jamal was moving quickly toward the cafeteria exit.

He sat hunched over a microfilm screen in the main branch of the New York Public Library. There was a blur of black and white images as he raced toward his destination. He stopped on a *New York Times* news article, from 1954. It was titled "Author William Forrester receives Book-of-the-Year Award."

The same photograph that was on the back of Claire's book was tucked beneath the headline. Jamal raced through the article. "Born in Scotland," he whispered to himself, "in 1930." That explains the accent, Jamal thought. "Moved with his family to New York in his late teens. Mr. Forrester does not grant interviews. He did not attend the awards ceremony, and was unavailable for comments."

"Yeah—I'll bet he was," Jamal said.

An hour later, Jamal was knocking on Forrester's door. There was no peephole greeting this time—Jamal knew that except for the Ivy League guy who made regular deliveries, he was the man's only visitor. The door swung open and Forrester filled the opening. There was the usual look of displeasure clouding his features, though it now seemed subtler, less pronounced.

"So," he grumbled, standing aside so that Jamal could enter. "I see we've now decided to make these visits a habit."

Jamal moved to the middle of the living room. He stared at Forrester and began bouncing the basketball, left hand, right hand, between his legs, behind his back, never taking his eyes off the man. It was an act of defiance; he felt tricked by the older man. In a curious way, used and disrespected. "You said you knew I'd be comin' back," he said at last.

Forrester glared at the basketball until Jamal stopped dribbling. He returned Jamal's glare with a look that was impassive and cool.

"I thought you meant once."

Jamal removed his windbreaker and started to toss it on a nearby chair.

"Hang your coat up. Please."

Jamal hung it on a wooden coatrack beside the door. He then walked up to Forrester's desk and sat on his basketball as he unzipped his backpack.

Forrester eyed him curiously. "You seem in a strange mood today. Are we feeling a little contentious?"

"I need some help with this thing they got the kids workin' on at the new school. If I go, I'm starting the semester late. I'll need to catch up."

Forrester stood at the liquor cabinet pouring himself a generous splash of scotch on the rocks.

"Ah, yes," he said, his back to Jamal. "The . . .*thing* . . . at school." He swirled his drink with a finger. "And what. . .*thing* . . .might we be talking about?"

Jamal pawed through his backpack and pulled out the school's paperback copy of *Avalon Landing*. "This," he said, and tossed it on the table. He studied the older man, waiting for a reaction, but Forrester was cool, he had to give him that.

"You ever read it?"

Forrester spun the book around so that the title faced him. Still no reaction, no expression.

Jamal said, "It's tough. I was readin' it on the subway comin' home. I'm tryin', man, but I can't get by the first ten pages."

Forrester flipped the book open with his non-drinking hand. He read for a moment, then looked up. "As I recall, it took me a while to get by those pages as well." He thumbed through the book. "Look at this," he said, shaking his head. "You dog-eared some of the pages. You never do that to a book—any book. Never bend the pages. Show some respect for the author."

An uncomfortable silence came between them as Forrester handed the book back to Jamal, the offending page smoothed down.

"I've made a friend at Mailor-Callow during my visits," Jamal said. "A very nice girl. Her name is Claire Spence."

"And why are you giving me this random piece of information?" Forrester said impatiently.

"Not random," Jamal said. "She showed me her valuable copy of *Avalon Landing,* a first edition. Has the 'A' on the copyright page."

Forrester blinked, his first show of discomfort. "I know."

"And even more valuable, a photograph of the author on the back jacket. Since then, he's never allowed his picture to be taken."

Forrester sipped his drink, not taking his eyes off Jamal. "I know that, too."

Jamal smiled, caught in the staring contest. "Of course I recognized you. Forty-five years younger, somethin' like that—but you. You're William Forrester."

The old writer turned and walked to the window. He stared out but said nothing.

"I've read the book many times," Jamal said. "It's—"

"I *know* what it is," Forrester interrupted. "The last thing I need is another person trying to tell me what *they* think it is."

"I wasn't gonna say that. I wasn't gonna interpret your stupid book."

"Oh? And just what *were* you going to say? That you're angry because I didn't tell you everything about me?"

"I told you about me."

"Well, you could learn a little something about holding back." He took a larger swig of his scotch.

"You like that stuff?"

"I wouldn't drink it if I didn't. It's the writer's friend—and enemy." Forrester cleared his throat nervously and ran a hand across his forehead. "What if I asked you not to say anything? Anything to anybody—and I mean anybody?"

"I won't."

Forrester nodded, jiggling the ice in his glass.

"And if I asked you to keep helpin' me with my writing?"

Forrester regarded Jamal, a deep vertical line etched between his eyebrows as he frowned. "Is this an attempt at blackmail?"

Jamal grinned, moved around on the basketball, and said, "It's an attempt to keep learnin' from you, that's all it is. I keep your secret whatever you do, man."

"Okay," said Forrester, finishing his drink. "Here are the ground rules. Do you remember our discussion about good questions and bad questions?"

"Sure. I remember."

"There will be no questions about me, my family, or why there's only one book. Those are bad questions. And you are never, *never* to say a word about this—where I live, what we talk about—to anyone. Agreed?"

"Agreed."

Forrester searched his eyes; Jamal did not look away. "Life has taught me that to trust is to court disappointment, occasionally even disaster. I try to avoid them both. I hope this is something I can trust you on."

"You got my word."

Forrester looked shaken. His anonymity had been blown, and by a high school boy he barely knew. But at least a bright and talented boy, he consoled himself as he walked to the liquor cabinet to refill his glass. He planned to get very drunk tonight.

Jamal pulled himself up from the basketball, knowing the time had come to leave. He had gotten what he came to accomplish—an arrangement.

At the door, however, he couldn't resist asking, "What's it feel like?"

"What does *what* feel like?"

"You know, writin' something—the way you did. That particular book."

Forrester stood silent at the bar, all movement arrested. Without turning around, he said, "Find out."

Later that night, after a two-hour stint of writing, Jamal decided to catch up with Fly, Kenzo and Damon at a small neighborhood restaurant where they often hung out. Fly had called earlier to say they would be there around ten. The lighting was poor in Pedro's Place, and many of the tables stood on shaky legs, the music was not to their taste—a lot of Spanish numbers, marimba, salsa—but the cook and owner, Pedro Ramirez, made dynamite burritos, enchiladas, and red beans and rice, gave free refills of soda and always took something off the bill. The boys speculated about him; he wasn't married and he had a delicate manner and used his hands a lot when he talked. But they eased off on the gender question because he was such a generous guy and an outrageous cook.

Fly, who had already consumed two burritos, was chewing on a toothpick. "Knicks are one up and Chicago's got less than a second—like point eight seconds—to get off a shot."

"This is the Garden?" Kenzo asked.

"How come every time I try to tell you somethin' like this you're always askin' questions?"

Kenzo, whose black leather jacket now featured Duke's collar hanging from the zipper, shrugged. "I'm just trying to picture it, man. Blue court? Red court? It makes a difference."

Fly leaned his chin on a fist, looking pained. "You think the Knicks could be one up in Chicago?"

"I don't know," said Kenzo. "That's why I asked."

"So anyway," said Fly, "they're in the Garden—okay? And they toss it into the—"

"M.J.," said Damon.

"Yeah, and Jordan dribbles two, maybe three times, gives this head fake—"

"This is happenin' in less than a second?" Kenzo interrupted.

"Hey, Kenzo, are you gonna let me tell the story or what?" Fly said, raising his voice.

"Yeah, Kenzo," said Jamal, who had just walked in, "let the man tell his story." He grabbed a dish of fries from an empty table that hadn't been cleared yet.

"Hey, Jamal," said Kenzo.

"Yo, man," said Damon.

Jamal sat down. He was happy to be with his friends, but he felt a twinge of guilt. He knew that everything would change if he switched to Mailor-Callow, and in fact everything had already started to change because he had secrets from them now. He had William Forrester, their man in the window, and that could never be shared. His old secret life, his writing, had led him to Forrester and probably to Mailor-Callow, too, and would ultimately lead him away from his friends. He felt guilty and a little sad, but he was with them now and he wanted to enjoy the time they had together.

Fly said to Jamal, "I'm tryin' to tell lamebrain here a story, man, and he can't listen for two seconds."

"C'mon, Kenzo," said Jamal. "Fly's got a twenty-three story to tell you. Listen up, man."

"Up yours, Jamal," Kenzo said mildly.

"So Jordan gives this fake," Fly said, "goes up and hits the shot with his patented fade away."

"Shot that can't be defended," Jamal said.

"Right. And the horn doesn't go off till Pippen's been huggin' him for, like, it seems like a minute. And this reporter comes runnin' over, tryin' to talk to the guy who was runnin' the clock. But they tell him, No, man, you can't interview the dude at the table and he says, I don't want to interview him, I just want him to time the rest of my life."

"Outstanding story, man," Damon said, laughing.

Kenzo said, "Even M.J. couldn't do all that in one second. You made it up."

"Screw you, Kenzo."

"Hey, did you make it up?" Jamal asked Fly.

Fly grinned. "I ain't sayin'."

Kenzo and Damon, whose families lived in the same project, left a few minutes later, and after Jamal had a Coke he walked Fly to his apartment building, which was a block from his.

"You ever met anyone famous?" Jamal said, breaking the silence.

"How famous?"

"I don't know. Well, you know, somebody most people would've heard of. That famous."

"Nobody like that around here."

Fly paused at the entrance to his building. "So—you really doin' this new school?"

Jamal nodded. "I think I got to, Fly. I know my ma wants it. Though she won't come right out and say so."

Fly nodded, working to keep his cool pose. "Okay. But don't be missin' any of these Friday nights. We got to party together, man."

"Nothin's gonna change," Jamal said.

"Sure," Fly said.

The two old friends exchanged a glance—uneasy, almost furtive in all that it didn't express.

"Okay, later," Fly said.

"Later," said Jamal. He walked away, feeling Fly's eyes on him, palpable, full of sad weight. He forced himself to keep his eyes straight ahead.

Chapter 8

Jamal began his new life at Mailor-Callow the following week. He was assigned to a locker and given a key. The locker wouldn't open. He bent over, jiggled it around, sweat trickling down his forehead. He was nervous and his hand trembled. "Stupid keyhole is jammed," he muttered to himself, "or they gave me the wrong key. Great to be late for your first class." The harder he tried, the more frustrated he grew; he began jabbing the key at the hole. "Come on—*go in.*" The problem, for Jamal, was symbolic of all that could—and probably would—go wrong in this new environment. He didn't fit in, and he never would. Almost as a confirmation of his fears, four female students strolled by, and one of the girls, a frizzy redhead, inclined her head in his direction and said, "Guess they didn't give him money for clothes."

"Hey, Steffi, lower it," said one of the other girls. "He can hear you."

They tittered among themselves and moved on. Jamal pretended not to hear; he gritted his teeth and continued trying to insert the key.

"Dummy," said a voice close to him He looked up. Claire was at his side, grinning at him. He felt a surge of relief; at least he had one friend he could count on.

"Hey, Claire."

"Hey." She tapped him on the shoulder. "You here for good now?"

"Yeah, looks that way." He gave the locker a baleful glance. "Can't open the thing. Auspicious start, right?"

"I said you're a dummy." She popped the corner of the locker with the flat of her hand and it opened easily. "At least they look good, right? Like a lot of things around here."

"Thanks."

"I like your sweater," she said. "Tan becomes you."

"Who's somebody named Steffi?" he said. "A redhead. Short."

Claire groaned. "Stephanie Meyers. A bitch on wheels. Her father's a lobbyist in Washington for the tobacco industry. I mean, *yuck*." She studied Jamal. "Why? Do you think she's cute or something?"

"I was just wondering, is all."

She continued to study his face, looking for a clue to what he was thinking. "Well, gotta make class. You got Crawford first period?"

"Yes."

"Me, too." She hesitated. "See you at lunch?"

"Sure." They exchanged an awkward grin.

"Well, come on. We're gonna be late. The ogre doesn't appreciate lateness."

Two minutes to first class. Jamal grabbed his books and ran down the hall, following Claire. Professor Crawford's class was just starting as they raced in the room and took seats. Crawford, standing at the lectern, thumb inserted in the watch pocket of his vest, watched Jamal until he was seated.

Then he cleared his throat, an exaggerated series of "him-him-him" sounds, and said, "You'll be pleased to know that this year's writing competition has now been scheduled. For those who choose to take part, all entries must be turned in before the break—no exceptions. Which means you still have several weeks of procrastination left." Several of the students laughed, including Steffi Meyers, who sat in the front row. "Feel free, however, to experiment with a more proactive approach to the assignment."

At the end of the hour as the students were filing out, Jamal stopped, frozen, as Crawford called out his name. Jamal walked against the flow of students until he reached the professor's desk. Crawford picked up a file and opened it.

"Mr. Wallace?"

"Yes, sir."

"I had a chance this morning to review the file sent over by your former school." He stood looking down, studying the file with a frown. "Your test scores are impressive, not to put too fine a point on it—more than impressive. But your actual classroom work? Not impressive." He removed a handful of papers, indifferent work that Jamal had turned in without much thought of preparation. Days at Franklin High had been days to endure until he could get out on the basketball court and sweat out his frustrations. "Is this the level of work I should anticipate, Mr. Wallace?"

Jamal started to answer, but Crawford gave a dismissive nod of his head and went on, saying, "Because if it is, it will go a long way in helping me determine whether I should treat you as a student"—he cleared his throat, an ironic stuttering sound—"or someone who is simply here to pursue—how should I put it—other endeavors?"

Crawford sat down behind his desk and stared at Jamal over the top of his rimless glasses. "I'm not interested in glib answers, Mr. Wallace, concocted to pacify me. Your work will give you ample opportunity to respond." He gave Jamal a wintry smile and inclined his head toward the door. "Good day, Mr. Wallace. If you hurry you won't be late for your next class, as you nearly were for mine."

Jamal left without a word, his face burning with humiliation. He started up the stairs to his history class when a boy about his own age, his face bursting with freckles and long curly blonde hair, came up beside him.

"Hey, man, you handled that the right way."

"Yeah. How's that?"

"You didn't say anything. I was standing right outside the door, watching. Crawford's a total control freak, and if you let him do the talking you usually come out okay. What a windbag." The boy held out his hand. "John Coleridge."

"Jamal Wallace."

They walked down the hallway together.

"You got history next—Gribetz?"

"Yeah."

"Me, too. Gribetz is no prize, but next to Crawford anybody looks good."

"How many do say something to Crawford?"

"And actually pass his class?"

"Yeah."

"Not too many. If they actually challenge him, they usually end up in trouble."

"Thanks for the tip, man."

"No problem." Coleridge grinned. "Me, I'm usually in trouble."

Jamal's days quickly settled into a new routine, one that left him little time for his old friends. After school there was basketball practice, then the subway home to tackle his homework, which for the first time in his life challenged him intellectually and took time and concentration. After bolting a quick dinner, he would walk to Forrester's building, taking new pages of writing for him to review. Those sessions were the culmination of Jamal's day. Everything had begun to pale beside their deepening friendship.

Toward the end of Jamal's first week at Mailor-Callow, the boy and the man stood a few feet apart from each other in front of the massive bookcases. Both were holding books. After a moment, Jamal closed his and turned to Forrester, who was deeply immersed in a passage he was reading—so much so that he was mouthing the words. Jamal put his book back in its slot, but failed to line it up exactly with the rest of the bindings.

"Have you read all these books?" he asked.

Reluctantly, the old writer looked up. "Young man, I wake up about five each morning after getting up maybe half a dozen times to urinate which I certainly didn't have to do fifty years ago. So yes, I think I can manage a little reading time."

He noticed the book Jamal had replaced. Frowning, he reached out and positioned the book perfectly. Jamal rolled his eyes and grinned.

"We've been talking about your book in school," he said.

Forrester snorted with disgust. "People have been *talking* about it for a long time. And the worst is when I'm expected to comment on what I wrote. What I wrote is what I wrote, period. Once done, what more is there to say? I'm not in the business of providing *Cliffs Notes* for the lazy and the stupid."

Jamal flopped into a chair, his long legs hanging over one of the arms.

"This guy Crawford, my English teacher, he's really messed up on it. He says the guy who's having trouble after the war is really you. Everything's interpreted as symbolism for the problems you were having—with everybody. It's, like, he reduces the narrative to therapy."

"Robert Crawford?" Forrester said, his expression alert.

"Yeah. Anyway, I'm thinkin' to myself, his interpretation is all wrong, man. I think there really *was* someone else—that it wasn't you in the story."

Forrester stared at Jamal, stunned by his insight. But before he could answer there was a soft knock on the door. Still unsettled by Jamal's words, he walked stiffly to the door and slid open the peephole. He unlocked the door and, not even bothering to open it, headed back to the bookshelf.

The young Ivy League guy ducked in, carrying packages.

"Mr. Massey," Forrester said, not acknowledging his presence with so much as a glance. "Another trip to your favorite destination, I see."

Massey looked at Jamal, his eyes widening with surprise.

"My friend, Jamal Wallace," Forrester said. "He told me about your little discussion on German automotive history. Very enlightening."

"His discussion, actually," said Massey with a touch of sullenness. He squinted at Jamal again, his eyes beady and suspicious, trying to fathom what this black neighborhood kid could possibly have in common with America's foremost novelist—a man whom he, Kenneth Massey, editor for the book publishing company that had brought out *Avalon Landing* nearly fifty years ago, revered so much that he ran errands for the great man on his own time. A secret that, at Forrester's insistence, he shared with no one.

"William," he said, "I've got the three bags. I can just leave them in the hall, if you're occupied."

"No, no, come in. There must be at least another few minutes till the sun goes down and you begin your panicky drive back to Manhattan."

Massey smiled weakly, accepting the sarcasm as though he was used to it. He lugged the bags into the living room.

"Your mail's in this bag," he said. "Books and magazines in this one. And I brought you socks for the next two weeks— they're in this bag. All white cotton. I've also got your latest check from accounting. They're wondering if you cashed the last one, because it's still showing up as outstanding."

Forrester reached for the six-pack of socks and ripped away the cellophane. He pulled out a pair, tore off the sticky protective band, kicked off his shoes and removed what appeared to be a new pair already on his feet.

"So—if you don't need anything else. . . ."

"What sports pages did you bring me?"

"*Boston Globe, Chicago Tribune, St. Louis Post-Dispatch, L.A. Times*—and, oh yes, the *Washington Post.*" He ticked them off on his fingers.

"Good," said Forrester. "Best editor I've ever had. You give me real service, Kenneth, and I thank you kindly."

The young man smiled uneasily.

"But I'll never understand how a book editor under the age of thirty can afford a BMW."

"It's leased. I've told you that."

"Would you like to continue the discussion of German automotive history with my friend Jamal?"

"Got to get back, William. Cocktails with an author."

"Get him drunk."

"A her."

"Well, get *her* drunk. Get her good and drunk. Drunk writers are the best writers, because they can see around corners and then turn them."

"Got to go. See you in two weeks."

Forrester was busy tweaking the edges of his new socks and didn't look up as Massey left, closing the door softly behind him.

"Want me to lock the door?" Jamal said.

"Yes, thank you."

When Jamal returned to the living room, Forrester was tossing the sports pages on his desk. He then dumped a pair of used socks into a trash can beneath his desk. His manner had become preoccupied and moody.

Jamal said, "Why don't you give that guy a break and get your own stuff?"

"He enjoys running errands for the esteemed William Forrester. It makes him feel important."

"Oh yeah, I forgot. You never leave here."

"I go out when there's something worth going out for."

"Is Massey pledged to secrecy, like me?"

Forrester nodded. "A condition of our relationship. Otherwise he can be excused. He's a replaceable part."

"I guess I am, too."

"Jamal, don't fish. It's not becoming."

"You treat the guy like dirt."

"That's not your affair." The old writer lined some black pens in a neat row on his desk. Tell me about this professor of yours—Professor Crawford. How did it feel to have him telling you what you *can't* do?"

"The truth? It felt lousy."

Forrester moved over to his ancient Royal manual typewriter. "Then here's what we need to do. Let's begin the process of showing him what you *can* do." He nodded his head at the equally ancient Underwood typewriter next to him. "Sit."

Surprised at this new development and feeling a surge of excitement, Jamal edged over and sat down. He touched the polished, beautifully maintained machine. "You want to know something weird, Mr. Forrester?"

"I think you'd better call me William. It simplifies things. Fewer syllables. You were about to mention something weird."

"I've never used a typewriter before."

"Of course. You're a computer boy. Fingers fly glibly over keys so easy to the touch, corrections in the blink of an eye—nothing to it."

Jamal pressed a key. "Man—the pressure this takes. You need finger strength."

"And mind strength," Forrester said. "You'll get used to it."

"Have you ever used a computer?"

"One time. My publisher bought me a laptop a few years ago. I found that the words came so easily I closed it and never opened it again. I don't trust words that come easily."

Jamal typed a few trial sentences, beginning to get the hang of it.

Forrester, watching him, said, "Why is it that the things we write for ourselves are always better than the things we write for others?" He began to type. "Go ahead," he said, motioning impatiently to Jamal with his left hand as he typed with his right.

"What?"

"Write."

Jamal watched the older man typing at a surprising speed. "What are you doing?"

"It's called writing. Like you'll be doing when you start pushing those keys."

Jamal removed the paper with his trial typing and rolled two fresh sheets into the platen. He wrote his name at the top of the page, and the touch was still heavy, unfamiliar.

"You're not typing," Forrester said a moment later.

"I'm thinking."

"No, no, that's for later. No thinking. First, the heat of creation. Then the clear chill of analysis. Be sure the steps are in that order."

Forrester was suddenly in a trance state as his fingers flew over the keys. Jamal could only stare in wonder.

A few moments later, Forrester came up for air. "Put another way," he said, "you write your first draft with your heart—and you rewrite with your head. The first key to writing is to write, not to think."

After another furious bout of typing, Forrester ambled into the kitchen, muttering to himself. Jamal moved over to see what the old writer had written. The dazzling tapestry of words he had churned out in a matter of minutes caused Jamal to catch his breath. This was writing by a real writer. "Jesus," Jamal said under his breath. He sat in front of the typewriter and stared straight ahead. His hands were on the keys but he didn't press them. It was as though he was at the beginning of something, and that all the writing he had done until then was prelude. The real work lay ahead, and for the first time he was afraid. Did he have what it takes? Was he a real writer or just a pretender?

He looked toward the kitchen. "William—can I ask you something?"

A faucet in the kitchen turned on, then off. "Hmm?" Forrester came into the room and stood a few feet behind Jamal, who could feel the man's intense focus.

"Can you stop starin' at me?" he said, hunching his shoulders protectively over the typewriter. "It freaks me out."

"It bothers you? To have someone waiting to see what you're willing to give them?"

"But you told me the truest writing you do is what you do for yourself."

"And for me," Forrester said. "Right now, for me. You said you had a question."

"How do you know if you're really a writer?"

"You question yourself. You question your work. Then you work hard to make it better. All the others give up."

Forrester walked over to a file cabinet next to his desk, fished out a key from a metal ashtray and unlocked one of the drawers, sliding it open to reveal file after file of elegantly typed papers. Jamal got up and stood beside him. The files, he noticed, were dated by years. Forrester removed a set of stapled papers from the file marked "1964," and placed it on the empty leaf of Jamal's typewriter table.

Jamal stared at the manuscript. "What's this?"

"Sometimes," Forrester answered, "the simple rhythm of typing can help get us from page one to page two. Start typing this."

"But what is this?"

"It doesn't matter at the moment."

"What's typing this gonna do for me? It isn't mine."

"No one can type someone else's words for very long. When you feel your own words flowing through you, start typing them."

Jamal read the title on the top sheet: "A Season of Faith's Perfection." He started to read the first page and immediately felt the pull of the language. "When did you write this?"

"Remember our discussion about questions? That is not a good question."

Forrester settled back in his comfortable leather recliner, waiting. Jamal began to type, hitting the heavy keys tentatively at first, but soon his fingers were flying as the words piled on top of one another. When he stopped, it was nearly midnight. He turned to see that Forrester was asleep in his chair, his mouth slightly open, snoring softly. Jamal watched him for a moment, marveling that he was here with this man, that they had formed such an unusual bond. It seemed more like a dream than real life. Jamal quietly tucked the papers into his backpack, put on his coat and headed for the door.

Forrester's voice stopped him. "Whatever we write in this room, stays in this room. No exceptions." He opened his eyes, just a slit, and watched as Jamal returned the papers to Forrester's desk.

"Good night, Jamal." He closed his eyes and resumed sleeping.

Chapter 9

Sneakers squeaking, the collective breath and sigh of a sweat-drenching all-out practice game, zigzag patterns, hitting the cutter, laying up (no jamming the hoop at Mailor-Callow)—and over the din of constant movement, the screaming imprecations of Coach Garrick: "Let's push it now, men! Effort! Move your butts! *Effort, men!*"

A player tossed the ball to Jamal, and he gave a dazzling fake, suckering his opponent out of defensive position. Jamal glided easily to the basket and reversed, using his left fingertips to roll the ball in the hoop. Hartwell took the ball up the court himself and Jamal sprinted over to guard him. Having learned his lesson the hard way, Hartwell turned his body away from Jamal, the better to protect the ball from Jamal's quick jabs and probes. Hartwell faked a shot as he moved to his right, his favorite pattern, but Jamal didn't bite and was ready when Hartwell drove hard to the basket. Jamal slid in front of him, but Hartwell lowered his shoulder and slammed into him, sending them both to the floor.

"That's a foul, Wallace," Hartwell shouted.

"No way. I had the spot, man."

Hartwell got right into Jamal's face. "I'll let you know when you've got the spot."

"Crybaby," Jamal said in a voice too low for the coach to hear. "Talkin' the game ain't playin' it." He shoved Hartwell away and Hartwell shoved back, hard. Jamal pulled back his arm, about to take a swing, when Garrick blew the whistle. Both players held steady, except for the glaring looks, neither wanting to take the first step back.

"Gentlemen," Garrick said, "we have a season that begins in a week. If I see that kind of thing *one more time* you're benched, I don't care if you're both the second coming of Michael Jordan. We don't tolerate this kind of behavior." He pointed to the free-throw line. "Wallace, you shoot from there. Hartwell—go to the other end. Start shooting, and alternate. First to miss does thirty speed laps around the gym. We're gonna get some discipline around here."

They both began to shoot; the rest of the team looked on from the sidelines, knowing the coach too well to voice any rooting interest.

The shots were dropping, swish after swish.

"Nine, Hartwell," said Garrick. "Ten, Wallace. Ten, Hartwell."

The two boys were totally focused on the rim in front of them. The shots rained down, settling softly into the net.

"Seventeen, Wallace," the coach called out. "Seventeen, Hartwell." Both boys were glistening with sweat.

Garrick paced the sidelines, waiting for one of them to crack. Jamal's thirty-first shot rolled around the rim, hung in suspension for an instant, and finally fell. A collective sigh went up from the sidelines.

"Forty-eight, Hartwell. Forty-nine, Wallace. Forty-nine, Hartwell."

The coach held up a hand. "Okay—one more for each of you." He gestured to Jamal. With all eyes on him, he brought the ball close to his chest, raised it above his head and slightly to the right and calmly swished it. All net. For the first time he turned around so that he could watch his opponent. Coach Garrick nodded to Hartwell. "Your final shot," he said. Hartwell bounced the ball—once, twice, three times—took a deep breath, exhaled and released the ball. It nicked the front rim, hung in the air, then nestled in the net.

The players were applauding, whistling and laughing. "Soft touch," one of them said.

Garrick stood beside Jamal and Hartwell. "That was one of the most impressive displays I've ever seen on a basketball court. You both perform like that under game conditions, we're gonna have some year." He paused, studying them both. The two boys looked at the court, reluctant to exchange a glance. "Okay, shower up both of you. And no more nonsense, understand?" They nodded.

Garrick walked off the court to the locker room.

The two boys finally looked at each other.

"Nice shootin', man," said Jamal.

Hartwell did not change expression. "Let me tell you one thing, Wallace. We may have the same skin color, but that doesn't mean we're alike."

Without another word, he turned and walked away. Jamal watched him, expressionless. He would not give anyone the satisfaction of seeing his hurt and anger.

As Jamal was leaving school after practice, he passed by Professor Crawford's classroom. The door was open and he was sitting at his desk. He looked up and said, "Mr. Wallace?"

Jamal stopped and looked in, feeling a twinge of nervousness deep in his stomach. Early that morning, before classes started, he had shoved a manila folder under Crawford's door—a clean copy of his most recent work.

"Professor Crawford?"

"The paper you turned in this morning. It displayed quite a bit of improvement over your earlier work. You might say, a quantum leap."

"Thank you."

"Out of curiosity, how long did it take you to write it?"

"I wrote it last night."

There was a long pause. Crawford raised his eyebrow as he stared at Jamal. Finally he put his glasses back on. "Well—I have some things to finish up here. Good day, Mr. Wallace." He turned his body slightly away from the door, not inviting a response.

Somehow Crawford's praise, if that's what it was, left a sour note. It was as though he didn't believe Jamal was capable of good work. There was just a grudging acknowledgment that what he was doing now was an improvement over his work at Franklin. Disappointed, Jamal walked to the subway, bent over from the weight of his backpack and his thoughts.

That evening, Jamal and Forrester sat in two recliners, the largest of the three TV sets turned to "Jeopardy." Forrester was sitting upright, watching intently, while Jamal was slouched deep in his chair, using his basketball as a headrest.

The onscreen contestant said, "'Birds of a Feather', for six hundred."

"Vibrant in color," said Alex Treback. "Its name borrows from this Vivien Leigh character."

"What is the Scarlet Tanager," said Forrester almost before Treback could get the words out.

"What is the Scarlet Tanager?" the contestant said, after a slight pause.

Jamal spread his arms in a gesture of confusion and looked at Forrester. "What exactly *is* a scarlet tanager?"

Forrester got up, with considerable grunting and old-man slowness, wandered over to the bar, poured a large, dark scotch, plucked two cubes of ice from a silver bucket with silver prongs and dropped them in his drink. "The Scarlet Tanager," he said, "was once described in these words by a writer you've never head of—'Thy duty, winged flames of spring, is but to love and fly and sing.'" He picked up his drink and returned to the recliner, sinking into it with a sigh. "He was writing about the bird's song—a song of new seasons and of new life."

His eyes glued to the TV, Jamal said, "James Russell Lowell." Then to the TV set he added, "I'll stick with poor assumptions for eight hundred, Alex."

Forrester looked over at Jamal, grinning slightly. "Well, I am astonished. You do have the capacity to amaze me, you know."

Jamal said, "You ever seen any scarlet tanagers around here? I mean, with the whole sky to fly in, why would they pick this dump?"

"They don't stray that far from parkland," said Forrester. He sipped his drink, regarding Jamal. "So . . . your professor wasn't exactly overflowing with praise this afternoon."

"Not exactly."

"And am I beginning to detect a bit more interest in the academic side of things?"

"Yeah, I guess."

During the commercial break, Jamal quickly surfed the channels, clicking rapidly. "Mailor-Callow doesn't give you much choice."

"There's something you need to know about Robert Crawford."

Jamal glanced quickly at the older man, his eyes suddenly alive with interest. "What?"

"He wrote a book, a few years after mine. And when he shopped it to my publisher it was rejected—which was the right decision. So instead of trying to write another book, he took a job teaching others how to write."

"How do you know that—about the right decision? Did you read it?"

Forrester waved off the question impatiently. "Not important how I know. Just keep in mind that when it comes to teachers bitterly disappointed in their own pursuits—well, those teachers can either be very effective . . . or very danger-ous." Forrester stood and stretched, and Jamal could hear the sound of cartilage grinding. "Our little break is over now. You've got an hour's more work to do."

Jamal sat at the ancient Underwood and Forrester leaned over his shoulder watching every word, resting one hand on his desk, the other on the back of Jamal's chair.

"There's an echo phrase here from the page before," Forrester pointed out. "That's good. Don't be afraid to repeat things when you're convinced the repetition works—even word-for-word. Remember, 'Bolero' has great beauty of its own as it circles around and around itself."

Jamal nodded, not saying a word, absorbing the lesson.

Slouching, bent forward under the weight of his backpack, Jamal headed home through the paper-littered, noisy, mid-night-populated streets of his neighborhood. The street-corner loungers were out in force, along with the dealers, the whores and the gamblers, who had their card tables set up on the side-walk. Midnight was not a somnolent and sleepy time in Jamal's neighborhood—three police cars sped by, lights flashing, sirens wailing, followed, half a block behind, by an ambulance, its siren also blaring. *Typical night in the 'hood,* Jamal thought. *But why should it be any different from any other nights? Traffic lights break here and stay broke for weeks. Get a bad snowstorm in the city, we're the last to get plowed out, last to get our garbage picked up—always last on line. Still in the back of the bus. Jamal walked at a steady pace, eyes straight ahead. Watch bad eye contact, man. Stay out of trouble.* On Jamal's face as he walked and mulled over things was an expression of sad awareness.

He tiptoed to his room, hoping not to wake his mother, and lay fully clothed on the bed. He read, for maybe the hundredth time, the last chapter of *Avalon Landing*. Forrester had man-aged to pull off pure magic, and like all good magic it was impossible to see behind the scene and catch the mechanism at work. Jamal had tried again and again, and he was still in the dark, captivated by the mysterious and beautiful prose but clueless as to how Forrester had managed to achieve that creative level.

He heard a noise and, looking up, saw his mother in her bathrobe framed in the doorway. For some reason—unusual for him—he had left his door slightly ajar.

"Did I wake you, Ma?"

"No. I've been awake."

She looked uncertain and, reading the look, he said, "You can come in."

"Really? Well, *that's* a first." She took a step inside and leaned against the door.

"I don't feel the need—I don't know—to hide things now. You know I write."

"Yes, I know."

He grinned. "You're a snoop, Ma. Been in here, haven't you? Snoopin' around, right? C'mon, admit it."

She looked flustered. "I've tried to honor our—well, our understanding, I guess you could say. But I'm a mother. Are you angry?"

"No. You did the right thing. I coulda been building a drug dynasty in here."

"You still readin' that thing?"

She approached the bed and sat on the edge.

"It's one of the books from school."

Mrs. Wallace took it from him and examined the cover. "*Avalon Landing,*" she said. "I've heard of it. Isn't he a famous writer—like Hemingway or Stephen King?"

"Yes. Like Hemingway."

"When I was a little girl, I loved to read. You couldn't keep my nose out of books. I was so proud when I got my first library card. But—somewhere along the way—I don't know—

there were so many other things that took up my time. I had to help out takin' care of your Uncle Henry and Aunt Clarise. My mama had to work. I'm not sure she even liked it when she caught me with a book. To her, it was like wasting time."

Mrs. Wallace opened *Avalon Landing* to the page Jamal had marked with the front half of a match folder. "Two eighty-eight. You're almost finished."

"I'm reading the ending, Ma. I've read it a few times."

She handed the book back.

"What's it about?"

"I guess you could say, I guess it's about how life never works out—at least not the way you ever meant it to. But you keep goin', you learn, you suffer, you shore yourself up. I guess that's what he's saying."

"I don't have to read a book to know that."

Jamal waited a moment, watching his mother closely, before saying, "You ever sorry? You know. . . the way things turned out?"

Mrs. Wallace leaned toward her son and kissed him on the forehead. "Not with you, baby. Never with you."

She took the book from him, placed it on the nightstand, an old carpenter's box Jamal had found in the street years earlier, and turned the light off.

"Let's have you try getting a good night's sleep for once."

In the darkness, Jamal stared at the ceiling, wide awake, his mind racing. *How did he do that ending? How did he bring all the pieces together just that way? I've got to know. Until I know, I'm still on the outside looking in.*

Chapter 10

On opening day of the Mailor-Callow basketball season, Jamal got to school half an hour before the start of classes. Again, Crawford's office was locked. Jamal smiled; he tried to avoid the professor whenever possible. There was a bin outside his office, on the wall adjacent to the door. It was crammed tight with manila folders—assignments that had already been turned in. Jamal tucked his own folder in the back, and said under his breath, "Let's see what you have to say to this, Mister Professor." He grinned more widely and even hummed to himself as he made his way to the cafeteria for orange juice and coffee.

The day dragged by. Jamal's thoughts kept dwelling on the game that night. He knew it was important to make a good first impression as an athlete, because being black, being poor, it was as an athlete that he could hope to gain acceptance. The school, too, was banking on his ability as a basketball player to take them all the way in their conference. Coach Garrick in recent practices had made it obvious that Jamal was his first offensive option. But what about his mind? Did the school really care about his academic gifts? Yes, his brains mattered, but his speed, court savvy and jump shot might just matter even more. He knew that and, with Claire's help, had begun to accept the reality of the situation. He would take from it all that he could get, with no regrets.

In the locker room that evening Jamal laced his shoes in a tight double knot, listening to the hubbub of players' voices. His shoes were older and more soiled than those worn by his teammates. He tried not to let it bother him. The dull, pulsing sound of the crowd gathering in the gym seeped through the walls.

A few minutes before game time, the players formed a circle, their heads touching at the center. Hartwell, the team's captain, put his hand in the middle and the rest of the teammates' hands joined his.

"All right," he said, looking at the other faces but quickly sliding off Goffrey's. "This is step one tonight. No thinking ahead. We play this game like it's the last one. Let's get it done. On three—one . . . two . . . *three* . . ."

They all yelled, "Maaay-looorrrr . . . *go!*"

Hartwell shoved open the door and they jogged up the tunnel and were suddenly surrounded by lights, noise and a packed gym. The band broke into a fight song. Jamal glanced around, blinking rapidly, dazed by the collegiate atmosphere. His heart was beating rapidly and beads of sweat formed on his forehead. He took his position, flexed his legs and thought, *This sure ain't Franklin, man. They got this on cable hookup. This is something else.*

The referee whistled, threw the ball into the air and the two centers jumped. Ball to Mailor-Callow. The small forward, Carl Morrissey, dribbled slowly up the court. Jamal broke for the basket, running a zigzag pattern, and lost his defender. Morrissey threw a perfect pass, finding Jamal mid-stride. He caught the ball and laid it in, stifling the impulse to kick off the game with a tomahawk stuff, a la Latrell Spreewell, a hero in Jamal's 'hood. The crowd roared.

The game was on. Jamal's fears dissolved in the flow of the action. He had all of his game tonight and he knew it, playing easily within himself. The basket looked a mile wide—how could he miss?

The opposing team, Trinity, was never in the game. Mailor-Callow, who had lost twice to them the year before, won by fifteen points. Jamal was high scorer with twenty-six, and was also high with nine assists. In every way it was the game he had hoped to have—capturing the flow and connecting with his teammates.

When he showered and left the locker room, a lot of his classmates who had not paid him the slightest attention were now coming up, smiling, joking, wanting to be his friend. Celebrity status had come his way overnight. Jamal was secretly amused. Mr. J. Wallace, Mr. Popularity. A jump shot and a few cool moves could do wonders for your personality.

He spotted Fly in the crowd of well-wishers, hanging back, and made his way over to his old friend.

"Hey, man. Glad you could make it."

They did the buddy shake. Fly grinned. "Twenty-six big ones, man. Eight from the floor, ten for ten from the line. A bunch of steals—"

"Only three, man."

"I mean, no way was I gonna miss this."

"It was all right, huh?"

Fly nodded enthusiastically. "You were doin' some serious investin' in that hoop, man." His expression, usually so jovial, showed some strain. Jamal knew that his friend was intimidated by the surroundings; even after a month at Mailor-Callow Jamal himself was still felt somewhat awkward and alien.

"I was kinda hopin' Damon and Kenzo would come," he said. "I asked them."

"They got tied up," said Fly, avoiding Jamal's eye. "So the plan is, the guys, most of the playground group, they're goin' to Nick's in about an hour. Friday night doins', man. I told 'em we'd catch up."

Claire emerged from the crowd of students and rushed up to Jamal. She stood on tiptoes and kissed his cheek. "You plan on doing that every game?"

"It just worked out tonight." He flashed a self-conscious look at Fly.

95

"Yeah, I'd say it worked out, Mr. Modest." She looked at Fly, a question in her eyes.

"My friend, Fly Black. My main man. Fly, Claire Spence."

"Hi, Fly."

He bobbed his head, his eyes glancing quickly off her. "Hey."

"Were you at Franklin together?" she asked.

"We been together since kindergarten." He grinned at Jamal. "I used to protect this guy from the bullies."

"Untrue."

"True, man."

A group of Claire's friends yelled out, "Claire, c'*mon.*"

"I'm on my way," she answered. Then to Jamal: "Don't hold the bus up too long, okay? The driver's on a tight schedule." Claire and three of her friends had hired a private bus and driver for the evening; it would provide transport to Claire's family's house on the north shore of Long Island for an after-game party. The entire Mailor-Callow team was invited, along with Claire's closest friends.

She pulled away, walking backward as she said to Fly, "Nice to meet you, Fly Black. Any friend of Jamal's . . ." She grinned. "You know what I mean."

When the friends were alone again, Fly looked seriously at his friend. "What you workin' there, man?"

"Nothing."

Fly shook his head, unconvinced. "Nothin', my eye. That girl got the hots for you."

"Get off it."

"And my guts tell me you got the hots for her, man."

"Listen, man—this party thing. It's the first game on our schedule—it's like a tradition. They do it every year. If I don't go it's gonna look funny."

Fly's eyes grew small; he couldn't hide his anger. "Nothin's gonna change, huh?"

"Hey, don't be goin' off on this, man."

Fly shook his head and looked away.

"I gotta do it, Fly. Just this once anyway. I gotta fit in this place."

"Sure, man. Well, you don't wanta be holdin' up that bus, know what I mean?"

"You around this weekend?"

"I'm around every weekend. You know where to find me." He turned and walked away.

Jamal watched him go, then slowly turned and walked to the bus.

For Jamal, the Locust Valley estates the bus passed on the way to Claire's were like scenes from an old video he had once checked out of the library, starring one of those old-timey actresses with money in her voice—Katharine Hepburn or Merle Oberon. White columns fronting massive homes, rolling hills, vast acres, it was a dream of opulence. Forty minutes after leaving the school, the bus pulled into the long, winding drive-way of the Spence estate. Jamal wiped fog from the window so that he could take in everything. This was better than any movie; this was real. And sitting across the aisle from him, smiling his way occasionally, was the most beautiful girl in the world—Claire Spence, his new friend, whose parents actually owned this dream place. If he died at this very instant, at least he would die with a smile on his face. The bus came to a stop under a porte-cochere—a word Jamal remembered having read in an F. Scott Fitzgerald short story with a heroine who reminded him of Claire.

The bus emptied quickly and everyone trooped inside, noisy and spirited, eager to party. The living room alone was larger than Jamal's entire apartment. Again, it reminded him of a scene from a movie depicting impossible luxury. Alumni, faculty and several ball players milled around, and Jamal, watchful and tense, gravitated to a quiet corner. By now, a month into the semester, he was growing accustomed to being the only black face in a sea of people, but he was still uncomfortable; his palms still sweated. A middle-aged man in khaki pants, sneakers without socks, a gray sweatshirt with "Princeton" emblazoned across the front, and a blue blazer came up to Jamal. He was holding a silverish drink with an olive in a long-stemmed glass, and his blue eyes were glazed over. Guy's ripped, Jamal thought.

"You put on quite a show tonight, my friend," the man said.

"Thank you." Jamal accepted the man's hand, soft and remarkably smooth, and shook it briefly.

"Billy Polk," the man said.

"Jamal Wallace."

"God knows, Jamal, Mailor-Callow can use new talent. In my day we had an ace team, but lately it's been the doldrums."

"There are a lot of fine players on the team."

The man grinned—more of a leer. "I love modesty in young people. Aren't you drinking anything?"

"I was about to get a Coke."

The man lifted his glass. "Claire's father makes a dynamite Flyi."

Jamal smiled politely. "I'm sixteen."

"Oh, right. Of course. And in training," the man said with a grave nod. "We must keep you in shape at all costs, Jamal." He removed a business card from his wallet and handed it to Jamal. "Anything you need," he said, "give me a call, okay?"

"Sure, thank you." Jamal took the card and stuck it in his pocket.

"Keep up the good work, fella."

"I'll try."

As Billy Polk headed toward the bar with the stiff, mechanical movements of a practiced drunk, Claire came up. She was wearing a subtle fragrance that stirred unfamiliar feelings in

Jamal. He countered the feelings by appearing cool, almost blasé.

"I see you met my notorious Uncle Billy."

"He gave me his card."

"Uncle Billy's practically a billionaire. He owns the patent on some kind of plumbing fixture no bathroom can do without. Don't ask me what. I never understood it."

Jamal grinned. "Maybe I have a future in plumbing fixtures."

She returned his grin. "Excellent career choice. You can learn to drink Flyis with Uncle Billy and discuss which gin goes with which vermouth." She touched his arm lightly. "You want to get outside for a while?"

"Sure."

They walked along a path that cut through the back of the estate and sat on a marble bench next to a red clay tennis court.

"You play tennis?" he said.

"I play at it. If I lose I get angry and quit."

"I'm going to learn the game someday," Jamal said, a thought that until that moment had never entered his mind.

They could hear music from the house, show tunes carried lightly on the soft night air.

"What's it like living in a place like this?"

Claire shrugged. "I don't know. It's just a place to live."

"I can't imagine living here."

"I'm glad you came, Jamal." She touched his hand, then quickly withdrew hers.

"Where's Hartwell?"

"He never comes to these things. He isn't very sociable. At least with the school crowd."

"Maybe he feels out of place."

Claire laughed, a sweet and throaty sound that Jamal loved. "John? Are you kidding? Coming out here would be slumming for him—a crashing bore. He hangs out with a show business bunch of kids in Manhattan—his dad's some big shot music producer, and his brother Maurice is a close friend of Leo DiCaprio."

"Hartwell is just too high and mighty," Jamal pronounced.

"Amen." Claire glanced at her watch. "The bus will head back to the city around midnight, which means I get to cram tomorrow for this test on Monday."

"What test?"

"Oh, it's this. . . this thing on the Sherlock Holmes books. They've got us tracking down this completely worthless, obscure stuff—you know, like who introduced Watson to Holmes. I mean, who cares, right? They just give it to you because it forces you to read everything."

There was a roar of drunken laughter from the house.

"Sounds like the party's in full swing."

Claire smiled. "Yeah. Uncle Billy and his crowd love to party." She looked at Jamal and after a moment of silence said, "So this friend of yours. He says you went all through school together."

"Fly. I've always known him. We're like brothers."

"Do you think he would like me?"

Jamal grinned. "I hope not. Fly always gets the girls."

"Thanks for the warning," she said, blushing. "Were you born in the Bronx?"

"South Bronx, the projects. Fly and I ran the streets starting young, but our mothers kept us out of trouble. Mine put the fear of God in me."

"It must be hard," she said after a pause.

"What?"

"You know—new people, new school."

Jamal studied her, searching for what was behind her words. "It's not hard," he said finally. "I'll tell you what's hard. Hard is growing up in a place even the cops don't like after dark. And what's hard is knowing you're safe there—safe because the bad people know you've got nothin' to give them worth stealing."

"So it's a good thing you're here, Jamal."

"People here don't think I've got anything to give them either."

Claire touched his hand again. "Not true. You've got plenty to give." Suddenly she jumped up and clapped her hands, a wide grin on her face. "I've got a great idea. There's a ball in the shed next to the basketball court—an old red and blue ball. Doctor J. signed it for my dad. Let's get it out and play some one-on-one, man."

"You kidding? That ball's a collector's item."

"You afraid of me? Afraid to be beaten by a girl?"

"Sure, Claire. You got me petrified, girl."

Claire got the ball, shed her jacket and dribbled the ball toward the basket. With one swift swipe of his hand, Jamal promptly stripped her.

"Got to protect the ball with your body," he said as he moved forward. "Think of the ball as your little baby and you'll take better care of it. And never dribble high. It's an invitation to theft."

She put a hand on Jamal's chest, pushing hard as she tried to defend.

"No hand checks allowed," he said, grinning.

"Oh, come on," she said, starting to breathe hard. "I need a handicap."

Jamal dribbled right, switching hands. "Right, right," he said in a teasing singsong. "Man's leaning right and he goes. . . ."

"Left!" Claire cried out in dismay, losing him.

But at the last moment, he swiveled back to the right, jumped and swished. "Man goes *right.*"

"C'*mon,*" she said, "it isn't fair. You're a foot taller than me."

"Still gotta play some defense. Watch the eyes. Eyes give things away."

"Like love and hate."

"No, more like right and left."

"So how do I learn to play defense, smarty pants?"

Jamal tossed her the ball. "Turn around." He reached for her shoulders and eased her around so that her back was toward him.

She felt his touch with a rush of heat. "What am I supposed to do?"

"Just try and get around me."

As she started to dribble the ball, Jamal reached out and placed his hand softly on the small of her back.

Claire, flustered, flinched away from him.

"What are you doing?"

"Back up. Feel that?"

"I feel it."

"The thing is, I can tell which way you wanta go." His fingers pressed gently. "Go ahead."

"Go ahead and what?"

"Try and get around me."

Claire's concentration was shattered by his touch. She had pretty much stopped thinking basketball strategy and was thinking Jamal and his hands, Jamal so close to her, and his touch. Forcing herself, she hesitantly moved left, but he pressed his hand slightly to that side. When she tried to go right, the same thing happened. Finally, completely frustrated, she bounced the ball off her foot and it rolled onto the grass.

"Sorry . . ."

"It's okay."

Jamal casually ran after the ball, and as he returned, a voice called out from the house. "Claire!"

"Daddy?"

"Some of the guests are leaving. The bus is loading up."

"Okay," she shouted back. She grabbed her jacket and turned to Jamal, her face flushed. "I'll see you Monday, okay?"

He nodded. As he and Claire walked up to her father, Dr. George Spence, the renowned heart surgeon, Jamal sensed the man's subtle dominant look, which said to Jamal as clear as any words: I am the man, and she is my daughter. Don't ever forget who I am and who you are. It was an aloof look that Jamal had seen in the eyes of many white men—a look he hated.

As she approached the house with Dr. Spence, Jamal called out, "Claire?"

She stopped and looked back.

"It was Stamford."

She looked confused. "I'm sorry?"

"At this bar in London," Jamal said. "He's the guy who talked to Watson about Holmes."

"Really?" Claire beamed. "Thanks, Jamal."

"Just thought it might save you time over the weekend."

He gave Dr. Spence a long, expressionless stare, then turned and walked to the bus.

PART TWO

Chapter 11

Winter came early, a snowstorm in November, followed by a blizzard in early December. Jamal was hardly aware of the weather: His days were so full they left him little time for reflection on life around him. He had gained more acceptance at Mailor-Callow than he would have ever thought possible; classmates invited him to parties, wanting to be his friend. But he had no illusions. Without basketball (he had emerged as the team's star, replacing John Hartwell in that role), and without his close friendship with Claire, he would just be "another smart ghetto boy on scholarship, tolerated and condescended to and always on the outside." When he used those very words to describe his situation to his mother, she had shouted at him angrily, calling him a spoiled ingrate. "And you're to never use the words 'ghetto boy' in this house again!" His gentle mother had risen up in wrath, and he had been mortified.

As much as the school engaged him, and intent as he was on excelling academically, his real life was his secret one, with William Forrester. Rarely an evening went by that they weren't together, talking, writing, discussing the craft. One evening in mid-December, they were hard at work, oblivious to the fat snowflakes falling outside Forrester's window. The old writer was pacing back and forth, reading from Jamal's notebook, while Jamal sat at the antique table beside Forrester's desk, papers strewn all around him, making corrections. Neither of them had spoken in nearly an hour when Jamal broke the silence as he gestured at the papers in Forrester's hand.

"You know how long I've been workin' on that?"

Forrester glanced up over the top of his glasses. "There's a reason it's called 'A Season of Faith's Perfection.'"

"Yeah, well it feels like it's been *two* seasons."

Forrester continued pacing and reading, intense and focused.

Jamal watched him. "You're in that place right now where you can't even hear me, aren't you?" No response. "I could ask you why you never moved out of this horrible neighborhood and you wouldn't get angry at me for breakin' our rules, right, William? Am I right?"

Jamal grinned and shook his head as Forrester went on reading, muttering something under his breath.

Finally Forrester looked up. "Paragraph three. You started a sentence with a conjunction—'And.' A conjunction at the beginning of a sentence is a sign the sentence should have been connected to the one before."

"Not always."

"What do you mean, 'not always?' It's a basic, very firm rule."

"You're foolin' with me."

"No, I'm not."

"In *Avalon Landing* you broke the rule left and right. You made up your own rules. A computer grammar check on that novel would green-line just about every sentence."

"We're not talking about *Avalon Landing*. But for argument's sake, let's say you break the rule. What's the risk?"

"Doing it too often," Jamal answered. "It's distracting and can give your prose a run-on feeling. But for the most part, the restriction against beginning a sentence with 'and' or 'but' is based on a shaky grammatical foundation, one that's still taught in too many schools by too many professors. Some of the best writers have been ignoring that restriction for a long time—including you."

Forrester smiled. "I could have given that little lecture myself, in those very words."

"You have."

"I would only add that you should break rules with intent. You have to know why you're breaking them. If a painter paints a tree that looks nothing like a tree, that's okay if, one, he knows why he's doing it that way, and, two, if he can actually paint a good tree. The tree that isn't there works better if the tree *could* be there."

Forrester flipped the notebook closed. "Jamal, this is your finest work. You have taken what was once mine and made it almost entirely your own." He dropped the notebook on the desk. "And nothing of value has been lost. Possibly value has been added. Apparently you've been listening these past few months."

Jamal couldn't hold back a grin of pleasure. "Praise from William Forrester," he said. "I can't believe what I'm hearing. I may faint."

"Don't."

"Listen, man, thanks for the words. They mean a lot to me."

"You should thank yourself—but you're welcome." Forrester sat in his recliner and sighed. "As for your little monologue when you didn't think I was listening, this neighborhood wasn't always so run-down. The placed changed, not me. But I was ensconced, had my own world here, and saw no reason to uproot myself."

"This neighborhood changed? I ain't seen nothin' changed."

Forrester frowned and hit the armrest with his open palm.

"You 'ain't seen nothin' changed.' What kind of sentence is that? When you're here, don't talk like you do out there."

"I was just workin' you, man. Sometimes home talk can provide home insights. If I were to say, 'I haven't seen anything changed,' what happens to the anger and stoicism? They dissolve in proper language. Home talk isn't available to everyone—but it is to me, and I'll always find uses for it."

Forrester listened intently and give a rare, brief snort of laughter. "You really are a piece of work."

After school the next afternoon, Jamal went to the main branch of the New York Public Library and walked up to one of the librarians, an older woman, who gave him a bright smile. "Can I help you?" she said.

"I'm tryin' to find a book—*Avalon Landing.*"

"William Forrester," she said.

"Yes, ma'am."

She typed quickly at the computer.

"Sorry," she said. "We have twenty-four copies, but I'm afraid they're all checked out. I can reserve one for you."

"No, that's okay. Thank you."

"Twenty-four copies," he informed Forrester the minute he walked in the door, a carton of Chinese food in each hand. "All checked out. I guess this Forrester fellow is another Grisham."

The dining room was set for two. Forrester was sitting reading a copy of the *National Enquirer.*

"Twenty-four? Did you get on the waiting list?"

Jamal put the food down on the table and dropped Forrester's change on the desk. "Why is it a guy whose book is still checked out fifty years later wastes his time reading a gossip rag?"

"What's wrong with it?"

"It's trash, man. You should be reading *The New York Times.*"

"I read the *Times* for dinner," Forrester said. "But this"—he tapped the paper—"is my dessert."

Jamal dished the food onto two delicate bone china plates and handed Forrester a set of chopsticks.

"Are you satisfied with my library research?"

"Twenty-four, all checked out." Forrester shook his head. "I've never really understood it, to tell you the truth."

"It's a great book, man."

"Compliments are not allowed in this house." Forrester looked serious.

110

"Listen," said Jamal, who was growing adept at shifting gears with the volatile writer, "they got this contest at school. This writing thing. You ever enter one of those?"

"A writing contest?" Forrester nodded. "A long time ago—and only once."

"Did you win?"

"Of course I won."

"Like money?"

Forrester stopped shoveling rice and chicken in his mouth, looked across the table, and said, "The Pulitzer."

"Oh," said Jamal, pretending to yawn. "Only that."

"Don't tell me you're thinking about doing it?"

"The Pulitzer? No."

"Don't be a smart aleck, Jamal. Is it something at school?"

"Yeah, and I don't think I'll enter. You have to get up and read it—in front of everybody. Not my thing."

Forrester broke a bread stick in half with an angry snap. "What does that have to do with writing? Writers write so that readers can read. A simple contract—nothing else should be expected of you. Let somebody else read it."

"You ever read from your book?"

"Never." Forrester pointed his chopsticks at Jamal and said, "You've probably heard of that coffee shop reading circuit, right?" Jamal nodded. "Do you know why they do that?"

"To sell books, I guess."

"No, no, there's a more personal reason. They do it to meet women. They couldn't care less about the dozen or so books they sign and sell, so long as one of those books belongs to someone wearing a skirt."

"You mean women will be attracted to you if you write a book?"

"Women will be attracted to you if you write a bad book. Writers are useless when it comes to most things not concerned with composing sentences. Most of them can't change a washer, pound a nail, read technical directions or balance a checkbook. But if they can write a novel, women come flocking."

"Did it ever happen to you?"

"Sure."

"Wow."

"But—as he uses a conjunction to start a sentence—it was a darn good book."

Jamal leaned forward and said, "Did you ever get married?"

The old writer stared at the young man. "Now that's not exactly a soup question, is it?"

"Sorry, man. I withdraw the question."

"Too late," said Forrester, surprising him. "As a matter of fact, I never did marry. But . . . I did learn a few things along the way that may be of help to you with your new acquaintance—this figment of your romantic imagination you call Claire Spence."

"Like what?" Jamal said, amazed that the old writer remembered her name and sensed his interest in her. He had mentioned her only in passing, and that had been weeks ago.

"The key to a woman's heart? An unexpected gift at an unexpected moment. It never fails." Forrester dove back into his food.

The next morning, Jamal met Claire at her locker after first class, a routine they had settled into and one that rarely varied, in the five-minute interval between bells. They exchanged quick gossip and made lunch plans or occasionally made an after-school date. Claire had given Jamal her home phone number—the private line in her bedroom—as well as her e-mail (she assumed he had a computer at home), but although he was tempted to call her when she filled his thoughts, it seemed too intimate a move at this stage. He was reluctant to push things.

"Let's go to the Soup Burg for lunch," he said. "My treat."

"Jamal—excuse me for sounding condescending, but you can't afford to take me out."

He grinned. "Order light, girl."

"I'll go under one condition."

"Always the conditions."

"We go dutch."

"But I invited you out."

"Dutch. Dutch or nothing."

"Claire—maybe you *are* condescending."

"Watch it, buster."

"I have a present for you," he said.

Her eyes widened in surprise and her face flushed. "You do?"

"I think you're gonna like it."

She pressed a finger to her nose and pursed her lips. "Now let me see. It's not my birthday. It's a little early to exchange Christmas presents. What's the occasion?"

"A whim," he said.

She nodded. "I see. Just a random thing." She glanced at her watch. "Bell's gonna ring. Catch you later."

Their lunch break was at eleven forty-five, early enough to get a booth at the Soup Burg. Claire ordered a grilled chicken sandwich and Sprite, and Jamal settled for a cheeseburger and a glass of plain water with a wedge of lemon.

"Well," she said, eyeing the package wrapped in newspaper Jamal had placed on the table.

"Well what?"

"You gonna give it to me? Do I have to beg?"

He shoved it across the table, and delicately, carefully, she began to remove the Scotch tape.

"Claire, it's only old newspaper. You're not gonna use it again."

"I know."

"Why can't women just tear the wrapping off?"

"Because we're women, not animals."

When she looked inside, Jamal could see puzzlement cloud her features. It was an old copy of *Avalon Landing*.

113

"Oh, Jamal . . ." She stared at it, but didn't open it. "This is—this is a surprise. Thanks." She was trying to generate enthusiasm.

"It's not a first printing or anything," he explained. "And it doesn't have a dust jacket—but, well, look inside."

Slowly, she opened the front cover. Inside was a sheaf of papers, folded and stapled.

"What's this?"

"Just something I wrote. Let me know what you think."

Claire smiled as she tucked them back in the book. Then she noticed the title page, with William Forrester's signature scrawled across the entire page.

"Oh my God," she said, raising a hand to her mouth.

"What?"

"What do you mean, *what*, Jamal Wallace? A signed copy. I've never"—she shook her head—"I can't accept this. I mean it must have cost you—I can't *imagine*. . . ."

"It didn't cost much. Really."

She brushed her fingers over the signature. "This is just the most wonderful thing. I've never had a better present. Never."

On the way back to school, they took a two-block detour, to Park Avenue and Eighty-fourth Street, so that Claire could show Jamal the building in which her father had his medical practice. She looked at Jamal, hunched over, hands in pockets. It was a cold day, hovering around the freezing mark, and he was wearing a windbreaker.

"Aren't you cold?"

"No."

"It's really cold. Shouldn't you be wearing an overcoat or something?"

"It's not that cold. Besides, I don't like to wear heavy stuff."

"That's my dad's office." She pointed at a large, red brick building. "Right inside the lobby, on the ground floor. He's here twice a week for consults and exams. Has a staff of six. He operates at Lenox Hill."

They started back to school.

"Is your father the one who talked you into going to Mailor?"

"I wouldn't say he exactly talked me into it. There was this one time, I might have been ten, eleven, I heard him tell my mother that considering my gender problem there was no way I'd ever put Mailor on my résumé." She smiled at Jamal. "Do you think I have a gender problem?"

"No way."

"He actually used those words. I'll never forget. You see, Mailor was an all-boys school back then. So—my father did what anyone in his position would have done. He got on the board and changed the rules. And every kid who walks through those halls knows that."

"Man, I call that clout," Jamal said, trying not to shiver.

Claire, almost hiding in her bulky coat, glanced up at him. "Jamal—that night at my house, after the game . . . Do you remember?"

"Remember what?"

"When we were, you know, when you were showing me some moves. . . ."

"Yeah?"

She stopped walking and turned, looking up at him. He stopped a couple of steps behind her. She moved closer. "Was it basketball you were showing me?"

Jamal's eyes skittered away from her insistent stare. "It was and it wasn't."

"Well, what *was* it, Jamal?"

He took a deep breath. "Whatever it was, it can't work."

"*What* can't work. You're talking in riddles."

"*That* can't work," he said. "The part that wasn't basketball."

115

"Why not?"

"Come on, Claire. I like you because you're smart. You know why."

"I do not. And maybe I'm not so smart."

"Well, ask your father. He'll explain it to you."

Claire started to grin. "Jamal—hel*lo*? I'm not asking for an engagement ring." She giggled, but couldn't draw a smile from Jamal, who seemed to be suffering an agony of embarrassment. "It was just a question, is all. Why does everything have to be so . . . black and white?"

"I forgot what the question was."

"Nice try, but I'm not buying it. You don't forget any-thing—Mr. Stamford."

He looked down at her and their eyes caught and held. He leaned close and kissed her softly on the lips.

"Was it that?"

"Yes, Claire."

"So is this—would you call it the defensive part of basket-ball?"

"No, more like the offense," he answered.

She giggled again and said, "I thought so."

As they continued to walk, their hands touching briefly, Jamal thought of Forrester's advice: an unexpected gift at an unexpected time. The man was clearly a genius in more ways than one.

Chapter 12

Professor Crawford had been following Jamal's progress at Mailor-Callow with great interest. He watched the boy take over the leadership of the basketball team, which was now leading its division with a perfect six-oh record. He had witnessed the boy's meteoric rise in popularity, his close friendship with Claire Spence, which, though Crawford fancied himself as a liberal, he considered slightly inappropriate. He had nothing against interracial friendships in theory, and if she had taken up with John Hartwell, for instance, instead of Wallace, Crawford would have understood. Jamal's presence at Mailor-Callow clearly unsettled Crawford. The boy was—insolent, not openly but Crawford sensed it in the boy. Could someone with his background, who had come to this school with an indifferent academic record from a public high school, be as bright and gifted as he appeared to be? Or was something else at work? It just didn't smell right to Crawford. The boy was just too good to be true. Crawford picked up Jamal's paper, glanced at it and shook his head. How could he possibly have written this? It was the best piece of work that had been submitted by a student in his twenty-two years at the school. Nothing else was even close. Something was fishy about the whole business, and when things were fishy Crawford liked to get to the bottom of them. He impatiently waited for Professor Carl Matthews, his colleague and best friend at the school. Matthews had published four volumes of poetry and, in his early fifties, he was considered one of the country's preeminent poets.

When Matthews appeared at the door, a large balding man with an engaging smile, Crawford waved him over to the desk.

"So what do you think?"

"It's terrific stuff, Robert. He impressed me without question."

Crawford drummed his fingers on his desk with nervous impatience. "Yes—but do you think he wrote it?"

"It's remarkable work," Matthews said, choosing his words carefully. "Did he do it without help? Did he crib it from somebody? Did he find a mentor to help him? I don't have a clue. It's certainly not anything I've read under another name."

Crawford continued drumming his fingers as he frowned at the younger man. "There's something about it—something vaguely familiar. I can't put my finger on it. But it smacks of something."

"Well, the kid does well in your class, right?"

"Actually, yes," Crawford admitted reluctantly.

"And I understand his test scores are through the roof."

"Yes, but test scores do not a writer make," Crawford said huffily.

"But maybe all he needed was some direction—and you gave it to him."

"Perhaps. But Carl, the boy's a basketball player—from the Bronx."

Matthews tipped his head back and gave a little laugh. "Writers come in all sizes and shapes—and colors, I should point out. There's no way of figuring it. There wasn't a book in my house growing up and I became a poet. Have you ever considered the possibility that he just might be that good?"

Crawford shook his head, his mouth a thin line.

"Not *this* good," he said.

Jamal saw Forrester every day now, a routine they both looked forward to and needed. Forrester let Jamal have the run of the apartment, as though the boy was a family member. It was an arrangement that brought comfort and a measure of excitement to both of them—the sixteen-year-old boy and the seventy-year-old man.

Two days after Jamal handed his paper in to Professor Crawford, he stood at the window staring through the lens of Forrester's video camera. A bird was perched in a tree limb across the street, but its features were indistinct. Jamal could tell it was small and brown, maybe a sparrow, but there was little to distinguish it from the milky haze of a damp evening.

"How do you focus this thing?" he called out.

Forrester was in the bathroom wringing out an old nylon shirt he had just cleaned in the shower.

"Just center on the subject," he said as he hung the shirt over the shower curtain. "Turn the focus ring a little to the right or left till it looks clear."

When Jamal got a clearer image, he panned away from the bird and focused on two attractive young women strolling along deep in conversation.

"Description?" Forrester shouted from the bathroom.

Jamal studied the two women. "Standard size." He paused and said to himself: "Standard to ideal."

Forrester walked in from the bathroom, wiping his hands with a towel. He moved to the liquor cabinet.

"Female," said Jamal, grinning. "Pretty sure of that."

He heard the chink of ice dropping in a glass. "You're getting the hang of bird watching, I see," Forrester said.

Tired of the game, Jamal placed the camera on a corner table. He turned and watched the old writer as he fussed with his drink.

"I was wonderin'," Jamal began.

"Wondering," said Forrester. "You don't have to drop your 'g's when you're with me."

"Wondering," said Jamal, who had grown used to being corrected. "If I asked you something and you didn't want to talk

119

about it—well, would you tell me you didn't want to talk about it and just let it go?"

Forrester, pouring scotch into his glass, said nothing.

"Or would you get mad at me for asking?"

Forrester still did not answer.

Breathing in deeply, Jamal said, "Did you ever try to write another book?" He could tell that Forrester's back stiffened. His hand shook slightly and he spilled scotch over the rim of his glass. He studied the pool of liquid before slowly wiping it up with the towel.

"I'm sorry," he said, turning to look at Jamal. His expression was impossible to read. "I missed what you were saying."

Jamal gave a little shrug. "It was nothin'—nothing."

"I've had it for tonight," the older man said. He picked up his scotch and towel and walked toward his bedroom without a backward glance.

But then, as Jamal picked up his backpack and started for the door, Forrester turned and tossed him a key. "Please lock up," he said.

Jamal stared at the key and then at Forrester.

"Is this for me to keep?"

"Good night, Jamal," Forrester said. "And remember to ask only the good questions."

"Wasn't that a good question"

Forrester nodded. "The key is yours," he said.

On Saturday, following a pickup game with his old friends, Jamal ate dinner with his mother and then walked over to Forrester's apartment. With a sense of pride, he inserted his own key and let himself in. Forrester was watching a tape of John Huston's *Beat the Devil,* one of his favorite movies, and drinking a very dark scotch. The first thing Jamal heard was the clink of ice as Forrester raised the glass to take a drink. The room was dark except for the flickering blue light from the set.

"Mind if I turn on a light?"

"Be my guest." The old writer's voice was thick and slow. Jamal could tell he was not on his first drink; probably not even his second. Jamal was getting used to nights like this.

He watched with Forrester as a strange man in a Nazi uniform strutted back and forth on the black and white screen, then he sat down in front of the Underwood and rolled in some paper.

After a few moments, Forrester walked, stiffly and with extreme care, to the liquor cabinet and made himself a fresh drink. He returned to the recliner, sat down with a heavy sigh, and punched the remote, turning off the television.

Jamal could feel his eyes on him.

"You know what the absolute best moment is?"

Jamal looked up but remained absolutely still. He sensed something important was about to happen and he didn't want to get in the way. Forrester got up and moved to the window and stared. He picked up a pair of binoculars, then put them back down.

"It's when you've finished the first draft, this precious prose and raw guts you've put your whole heart into . . . And then you read it. By yourself." His tone deepened and dropped in volume; he was no longer slurring his words. "For that moment in time, it's your book. It belongs to you. . . . Before the editors and the critics and everyone else take what you worked on for five years—something they couldn't do in a lifetime of trying—before they *own* it and think they *know* it. . . . And pick it apart."

He sipped his scotch and said, "Forget them all. They don't know anything about what it takes."

"People love that book, man."

"I didn't write it for anyone, you see—especially for the critics. And when they started explaining what I was *really* trying to say—well, that was a luxury I refused to give them twice."

121

"But that was fifty years ago."

"You have no idea what a short time fifty years is. You're too young to know. I haven't forgotten a thing. It all happened yesterday, the pain of bringing it to life."

"Yeah, but women go through childbirth, they have all that pain, and then they forget the pain and do it again."

"Nobody forgets pain, Jamal, and women never forget anything. You've got a lot to learn about women."

A few minutes later, Forrester slipped into a profound sleep. Jamal went over and nudged him. "William?" He was completely out. It was cold in the apartment—Forrester complained that he froze in the winter and sweltered through the summer months. Jamal wandered into Forrester's bedroom searching for an extra blanket to put over him. He turned on the light and checked the bed. No luck. He opened the first of two chest-of-drawers; it was crammed with white athletic socks. *Probably hauled out here,* Jamal thought, *by the Ivy League guy who called himself an editor.* He opened a second drawer and found a white woolen blanket. He reached to pull it out when he saw below it an open box stuffed with photographs.

"This is gold," Jamal muttered. He pulled out the box, sat on the side of the bed and started sifting through them. They were family photographs—mainly snapshots, indifferently composed, simply meant to capture the moment. The best kind of photographs because instead of calling attention to the craft, they revealed the people without self-consciousness, as they actually were. There were photographs of an older couple, Clayton and Emma Forrester, Forrester's parents (their names and the date, 1933, were on the back). But Jamal was particularly fascinated by the two boys who appeared together in picture after picture—two little boys playing in sand (Lake Michigan, near Lake Charlevoix, 1935, was printed on the back of one); two young boys beside a shiny black Packard convertible; two young men on a golf course—the boy holding a putter in the air and leering at the camera was a very young version of Forrester; two slightly older young men at Yankee Stadium wearing caps; the same two young men, from the same period, at a Knicks game. There was a photograph, dated 1951, showing Forrester in civilian clothes and the other young man in an army uniform. They had their arms around each other's shoulders.

"Forrester and his brother," Jamal said out loud. "It's gotta be."

He dug out another picture, this one of Forrester alone, dated 1954. "The year his novel was published," Jamal said to himself. He was wearing a suit and stood rigid, his features grim. This was the Forrester that Jamal knew, an uneasy guest at life's party. What had happened to the smiling boy?

Jamal put the photographs away and closed the dresser drawer. He spread the blanket over Forrester's sleeping form. He stirred but remained asleep. His desk lamp was still on and Jamal's manuscript was placed under it.

"A Season of Faith's Perfection." By Jamal Wallace.

Jamal turned a couple of pages, shaking his head, smiling. "Man," he muttered to himself, "this is *good stuff.*"

He glanced around, checking to see if Forrester was still sleeping, tucked the manuscript under his arm and clicked off the light.

During the winter months, Terrell worked one of the Madison Square Garden ticket booths. Jamal biked into Manhattan Sunday afternoon to pick up two Knicks tickets from his brother. Terrell tapped the keys of a ticket vending computer with one hand and used the other to point at a seating map.

"I can put you right here," he said. "You're lucky I've got these. Houston's not a hot ticket this year."

"Olajuwon's no longer a force," Jamal said.

"Whole team has aged."

Jamal pulled out some crumpled bills. "These are fine seats. Thanks, man."

Terrell punched a button and the ticket machine whirred and spit out two tickets.

"So who's the chick," said Terrell. "Gotta be a chick, right Romeo?"

"Guess I've just got to keep you guessin', man," Jamal said with a grin.

"I'm not sure this is a good idea," Forrester said. His face was flushed and his hands were shaking.

"William, you love the Knicks. You watch every game on TV."

"From my recliner. Best seat in the house."

"Come on, let's get a move on now. We don't wanta be late."

"Don't misunderstand me," Forrester said. "I appreciate all the trouble you've gone to and I know the Knicks are a hot ticket. Isn't there someone else you'd rather take? That girl you keep telling me about? Someone your own age?"

"Let's get going now." Jamal opened the clothes closet in Forrester's bedroom, which doubled as storage for more boxes of books and writing files. There were rows of empty hangers, along with two blazers, two pairs of gray slacks, one hat and one pair of dress shoes.

Without another word, the old writer slipped on the jacket and shoes and put on the hat. He turned to Jamal; one of his eyes was twitching with strain.

"It's still light out," he said. He reached in the pocket of his jacket and removed a pair of sunglasses.

"It's dark out, man. Nearly six o'clock."

Forrester put the glasses on.

"We stay together, understand?"

"I know."

"Crowds are a bit of a problem for me."

"Don't worry."

Forrester brushed his hand along the jacket and gave the brim of his hat a nervous tweak. He turned to Jamal. "Well?"

"You look good, man. I mean, it's not the newest stuff, but hey, who cares?"

"I wasn't asking how I look. I was asking if we're ready to go."

"Sure, we're off. Rockin' and rollin'."

Forrester walked out of the bedroom, leaving Jamal to close the closet door and turn off the lights. Jamal stared into the closet, at the rows of empty hangers, and shook his head. "Man," he whispered to himself, "you sure don't get out, do you?" He felt a surge of pity for this strange and brilliant man he had grown to love.

Forrester insisted they take a taxi into Manhattan.

"I don't like subways," he explained. "They're confining."

"Confining?"

"They also go too fast."

Jamal looked at his friend with surprise. "The four line? I've never been on a fast one."

Forrester nodded and gazed out the window. They didn't exchange another word until the cab arrived at Thirty-third Street and Seventh Avenue. Forrester shrank back as they got out of the cab. A large crowd had already gathered an hour before game time. The quiet and safety of Forrester's apartment were gone, replaced by noisy humanity; for the old writer the world was suddenly unpredictable and dangerous.

Jamal and Forrester walked along the concourse, basketball fans surging around them, raucous and spirited. The steady rumble of pre-game music seemed to make the arena vibrate. Jamal could sense Forrester's tension growing; he put a hand up to the side of his face as though to block out the sound. His face, usually ruddy, had taken on a clayish pallor.

Jamal gave him a concerned look. "You okay?"

125

"I'm fine," Forrester said grimly.

"We're playin' here in two weeks," Jamal said. "I can't tell you how down I am for that."

"Down?" said Forrester vaguely.

"Excited—you know. I guess every kid dreams of playing in the Garden."

Forrester didn't respond but walked stiffly on, looking neither to the right nor the left, as though by not looking at the crowd it would disappear.

"I said we're playing here in two weeks. State tournament."

"I'm hot," Forrester mumbled. "It's hot in here."

Jamal spotted a stand selling game programs a few feet away.

"Hang on, man," he said to Forrester, patting his shoulder. "Let me get a program. We can study the stats." Forrester was an avid reader of baseball and basketball box scores and liked any numbers associated with sports.

Jamal glanced away, and reached in his pocket for money— glanced away for only a second, but it was that awful second that can separate a child from his parents. When he looked back, Forrester was gone. Jamal frantically scanned the milling crowd, swinging his head right and left, but in that brief instant when he'd looked away the old man had disappeared, and Jamal felt a spasm of terror. Forrester was no longer the great American novelist, but a friend in Jamal's charge, a five year old who was lost, and Jamal was responsible for his welfare. He was suddenly the parent, Forrester the child, and he felt that overwhelming, sickening panic parents feel when their child is lost—even for a moment.

He gripped the program like a club and started to run through the crowd. "William," he shouted. "*William . . .*" At that moment the crushing sound of the pre-game introductions cascaded from the garden floor, drowning out his calls. Jamal jumped on the stand that was selling programs, paying no attention to the angry shouts from the vendor.

He kept searching and shouting, and finally spotted Forrester cupping his hands around his mouth, sweat beading on his fore-head and turning in slow circles. Jamal shouted, "William—*over here.*" He jumped down from the stand and shouldered his way through the wave of spectators still filing in. When he reached Forrester and grabbed his upper arm, the old writer was hyper-ventilating; he held his hands to his ears and flashed Jamal a look of stark terror. Jamal's own panic suddenly dissolved in sadness as he steered Forrester by the elbow to the nearest exit.

"Hey, man," he said, "it's okay. Take it easy now. Let's get outta here."

Forrester turned a dazed look on Jamal, as though he was staring at a stranger. Suddenly he shook loose from his grasp and scowled at him. "Leave me alone."

"I think we should go home, William. We'll try this some other time. Are you cool with that?"

Forrester sighed and slumped against Jamal's arm, defeated. They stopped for a minute at Terrell's ticket booth.

"Hey, my brother, we've got a little problem here. My friend isn't feeling too good."

"What's wrong with him?"

"Panic. He doesn't get out too often."

Forrester stood breathing deeply, his eyes closed. It was clear that he wouldn't move unless propelled by Jamal.

"This old guy a friend of yours? Some professor or some-thing?"

"Listen, Terrell, can you get off?"

"The game's starting and I have to tally up. Then I'm outta here."

Jamal leaned close and whispered, "You still got a key to the gate at the Stadium?"

Terrell looked puzzled. "Yeah. Why?"

"I want him to see it. He used to go to games with his brother. Man, I know this is asking a lot—I'll owe you big time."

"It's January, Jamal, are you nuts? Snow all over the ground, man."

"Do this one thing for me. I'll make it up to you."

Terrell hesitated. "How long is this gonna take?"

"Not long. Just a stroll, man. Soak up some atmosphere."

Forrester came out of his trance and said, "Who's this person?"

"My brother, Terrell. He's going to get us in Yankee Stadium."

"Now?"

"Tonight."

Forrester looked puzzled. "Is that legal?"

"I'm security," Terrell said quickly.

"I love the Stadium." Forrester had a dreamy look on his face. "What a wonderful idea."

The two young men and the old man emerged from the taxi in front of Yankee Stadium, vast and gray in winter shadows. The streets were practically deserted—no noise, no crowds. Forrester's breathing had calmed and once again he seemed in command of himself.

As they approached the side gate, Terrell moving ahead with the key, Jamal said to Forrester, "So you used to get out?"

"Yes. A long time ago."

"What happened? And don't tell me it isn't a good soup question. It is. A necessary question."

Forrester smiled thinly and nodded. "When you start to stay inside as I did, one week can become two. Two weeks become three. And before you know it, the weeks have become months. Time has a way of doing that."

"I'm sorry, you know, about what happened."

"No apology needed." Forrester added nervously. "Are you sure this is legal?"

"Come on, William. My brother's got the gate open."

"We can't stay long," Terrell said as they came up to him. "Don't want to get me found out here." He turned to Forrester, grinning. "I hear you're a Yankee fan."

"Joe DiMaggio was my hero as a young boy. Then Berra and Mantle. Now Jeter."

Terrell beamed. "Jeter's my main man," he said. "Follow me."

Once inside the stadium, the beam from Terrell's flashlight danced as they moved around to the first base side and into the Yankee dugout. Terrell handed the flashlight to Jamal. "Be back in a few. Got to make a couple calls." He headed back to the clubhouse.

"Watch those steps," Jamal cautioned Forrester. He stared out at the dark snowy expanse of the playing field, imagining spring and sunlight and players taking batting practice, hitting fungos, playing catch, playing pepper. He turned to Forrester. "Well, here we are—ground level. It's kind of exciting."

"Yes, it is."

"Ground level—the house that Ruth built. And Mick and Joe."

"And Berra and Guidry and the Scooter," said Forrester as though in a trance, a look of wonder softening his features. Jamal could suddenly see the boy in the old man.

After they stood in silence staring out at the pale snowy expanse, each caught up in his own thoughts, Forrester said, "Why did you bring me here?"

"It's your birthday, man. I mean, what can you get for the guy who's got everything?"

Forrester looked surprised. "How did you know that?"

"It's not that hard. You're a famous writer and your biography's out there, even though you've tried to hide it all your life. I just did research online." He paused, wondering how to proceed; he knew he was entering delicate territory. "I thought with all the games you saw when you were a kid—you and

129

whoever you saw them with—well, it occurred to me maybe you never got down this close."

Forrester peered out at the dark snowy expanse, so crammed with memories from another season of the year and his life.

"We were here almost every game that last summer," he said softly, "until he left for the war."

Jamal had to look away from the pain in the old writer's eyes.

"I thought it would be the same when he came back from Korea," Forrester continued. "But when Richard . . . my brother . . . when he came home, he was, well, he talked a little less and drank a lot more. And I promised our mother I'd help him through it."

Forrester shivered and crossed his arms over his coat. Jamal hardly allowed himself to breathe, fearing that the slightest distraction might stop the flow of words.

"So one night we were out drinking. I was a few drinks behind him and we were going at it hard. The dive in Portchester we'd driven to had a very liberal policy for lushes like us—they would let you drink all night, no questions asked. As we got drunker, we started to argue. *Avalon Landing* had been out about six months and was picking up steam. Richard accused me of having robbed him of his life by putting him in my novel. Writers often get accused of using people, to which I would reply, What else is there for a novelist to do? We use what we know, if we're any good. So the argument escalated and he decided to drive back to Manhattan. I said he was too drunk to drive and I tried to talk him into leaving the car out there and picking it up the next day. But he was too angry and drunk to listen to reason. The argument shifted to whether we would drive in or take the train. I opted for the train and left him there with a fresh whiskey in his hand." A sob caught in Forrester's throat. "I left him there. I walked out on him, my brother . . .the person I loved more than anyone in the world. I left him drinking in that bar." He had to stop; he wiped his eyes. "Because I was stubborn—because I was so stupidly stubborn. I could have driven the car. I didn't have a license but I knew how to drive, and I wasn't as drunk as he was."

Forrester slumped on a seat and held his head in his hands. "The ironies of life. Richard made it through the whole war and his brother left him in that bar in no condition to walk out of it steadily, let alone drive thirty miles into the city." Forrester began to sob into his hands. Jamal wanted to reach out and comfort the older man, but sensed that he was beyond the easy comfort of a touch or a hug. He stumbled on, saying, "The nurse . . . the next day . . . the nurse was typing out . . . this thing . . . and you know what she told me? *What she said to me?* She told me how much my book meant to her.

"My worthless little novel." Forrester bit off the words with disdain. "A bunch of words my brother was convinced had robbed him of his life. And he's getting cold a few rooms away, head mashed . . . partly gone . . . you know, pulp . . . through the windshield. I loved him more than anything and all she could talk about was a worthless stack of paper."

Forrester continued to stare out at the field, making no attempt to hide his tears from Jamal.

"That was when my life ended," he said.

Jamal couldn't hold back the words: "No. No, William. You're wrong."

Forrester didn't hear him, consumed as he now was with memories that had been locked inside him for so long.

"We would spend our summers here," he said. "And if we were lucky, a few weeks in the fall."

"And many of those falls you had the World Series," Jamal said.

"Not enough. Nothing can make up for it. Nothing could ever be the same."

"'The rest of those who have gone before us cannot steady the unrest of those still here.'"

Forrester stared at Jamal. "My words."

"The last chapter."

"And you knew the hero wasn't me."

"Somehow I did know that. Don't ask me how I knew."

Forrester, his eyes still glistening with tears, smiled at Jamal. "You are a remarkable young man." He turned and stepped up to ground level and walked out onto the field, his breath sending up trails of smoke.

Terrell entered the dugout from the clubhouse and slapped his brother on the shoulder. "This is all so weird, man."

"It's okay. He needs this."

"So how do you know this guy again?"

"He's my teacher."

"A strange dude, little brother."

"No, Terrell. He's a great man who's suffered through some hard times."

When Jamal got Forrester back home, he used his own key to open the front door to the apartment. Forrester looked more exhausted than Jamal had ever seen him, but at the same time there was a glow in his eyes, a look of peace as though he had been delivered from a burden.

"Thank you for a wonderful evening," he said. "This is one of the best times I've had in years."

"We had fun, didn't we?" Jamal grinned. "Rocky start, but then it all kicked in."

"Jamal, I've come to realize that if I give you enough time, you'll find new ways to amaze even me." He hesitated. "Does your brother know who I am?"

"No. Nobody knows."

"Do you remember when I asked if I could trust you never to say anything about me?"

"Sure. I remember."

"It appears that trust was well-placed."

"Does that mean I've passed the test?"

"What test?"

"The Forrester veracity test."

"You passed long ago. Good night, Jamal."

"Good night, William."

Forrester squeezed his shoulder. It was the first physical contact the old writer had ever initiated, and suddenly Jamal thought of his father—and thought of him without bitterness or resentment. It was a good feeling to be free of the dark thoughts he had harbored for so long. The old writer's touch meant everything.

Chapter 13

On Wednesdays Jamal did not have Professor Crawford's English class, but instead had study period, which was presided over by his homeroom teacher, Irene Davidson, who taught eleventh grade physics. When he arrived at school the following Wednesday, there was a note for him posted on the bulletin board that read: "Come see me in the auditorium first thing this morning." It was signed Professor Crawford, with an elegant flourish.

Jamal shouldered through the morning flow of students to a sweeping room, empty and dark except for the bright rays of sunlight streaking through the windows. Above the stage were about a dozen framed photographs of famous American authors—including the one of William Forrester that had appeared on the first edition of *Avalon Landing*.

Crawford's voice pierced the silence from a seat in the corner. "Over here, Mr. Wallace."

Jamal walked slowly to his table, on which was a stack of student papers and a cup of black coffee in a Mailor-Callow mug.

"I saw you glancing at the photographs," Crawford said, removing his glasses and rubbing his eyes. "Any favorite?"

"No, not really," Jamal answered, wondering where this was headed. Having grown up in the South Bronx, he had a nose for trouble. He sensed trouble now and was on the alert.

"Take a seat," said Crawford.

Jamal sat opposite the professor.

"I sometimes come here during free periods. Just me, the aspiring"—he held up a few of the student papers— "and all of the masters"—he gestured toward the photographs.

"There was a note that you wanted to see me," Jamal said.

"Indeed." Crawford swept the papers to one side of the coffee. He made a face. "I really have to teach the school a better brewing method."

Jamal waited.

"Mr. Wallace, I think it's time you and I had a very honest and very open discussion about your writing."

Jamal's street sense warned him that something was wrong, but he wouldn't give Crawford anything. So much of life in the projects was poker, bluffing and attitude. His expression was neutral; let the man make his move.

"I thought you liked my work," he said matter-of-factly.

Crawford turned on a thin smile. "It's professional, extremely expressive of feeling—full of color and nuance." He shook his head as though in disbelief, staring at Jamal intently. "No, Mr. Wallace, the question concerning your most recent work isn't whether it's good—of that there's not a doubt—but whether it's *too* good."

The professor sipped his coffee, waiting for Jamal to respond. But he offered nothing more than a slight lifting of his eyebrows, as though to say, It's your show, Professor, you called me here and I'm listening.

"The acceleration in your progress from your old school to this one," Crawford continued, "is unusual to the point that I'm faced with drawing one of two conclusions. Either you've been blessed with an uncommon gift that has just suddenly begun to flower—or . . ." He gave a shrug and continued to stare at Jamal.

"Or what?"

"The only other possibility that I can imagine, Mr. Wallace, is that you're getting—what should I say—inspiration from elsewhere."

Now the cards were on the table. Jamal looked at his hand and didn't like it. He would have to play his hand without help from Forrester, and if Crawford was dealing from the bottom of the deck, he would still have to find a way to beat him. First rule of the neighborhood: Don't go looking for trouble, but when it does come never turn your back on it, because it doesn't go away.

Crawford stood, tucking his work into his briefcase. "Given your previous education . . . and your background . . . given all that, I'm sure you'll forgive me for drawing some of my own conclusions."

"Like what? What conclusions?"

"I doubt it's necessary for me to spell it out, Mr. Wallace. Not with your test scores."

"I wrote those papers, man. Even with my background."

Crawford's features hardened. "Do not call me 'man.' I am either Professor Crawford or Mr. Crawford. We're not in the ghetto here."

"I don't live in a ghetto. Ghettos are in Europe."

"The point is, show respect."

"Sure, Professor. Well, Professor, I'll repeat what I just told you. I wrote what you have here. It's mine."

Crawford clicked his briefcase closed.

"Then I'm sure you won't mind showing me just what you can do. The next assignment is due in two weeks. I'll schedule some time for you to come to my office. I'd like to have you write it there."

Jamal nodded and started to leave.

"In the meantime . . . if there's anything you wish to talk about . . . let me put it this way. If there are problems, time will only make them worse."

He picked up his mug and briefcase, turned on his heel and left the room, feeling the boy's eyes burning into his back.

Jamal was too upset to make practice that afternoon. He pleaded a migraine—he'd suffered from them in the past and a susceptibility to them was listed on his health records—and went directly to Forrester's apartment. He marched in in a fury, reached for a can of soda in the refrigerator and slammed the door closed so hard he knocked a set of newspaper clippings from their precise formation on the refrigerator door. While he yanked the tab off the soda, Forrester put the clippings and magnets back in proper order.

"I'm sick of the school," Jamal said. "I'm sick of writing for people who don't care one bit about me or what I can do."

"Present company excepted, I assume."

Jamal blurted out his meeting with Crawford, then said, "Do you think if one of his fancy white rich kids handed in my stuff, he'd be questioning it? Would he raise any question about their background?"

"No, I don't. I think he'd love the work."

Forrester's answer stopped Jamal in the middle of his tirade. He regarded the old writer closely, looking for the polite lie.

"You do?"

"What has your professor stumped and more than a bit frustrated is Jamal Wallace, this kid he can't figure out. You're an enigma to him. What do you suppose people are most afraid of?"

"What?"

"Whatever they don't understand. When something is a complete puzzle, we come up with our own assumptions."

Jamal gave Forrester a weary sigh. "This is another lesson, isn't it?"

Forrester leaned in close, intent on making Jamal understand. He said, "Crawford has no clue how a poor black kid from the Bronx can write the way you do. Nothing in his background makes allowances for someone like you, so he assumes you're not who you seem to be. The writing is excellent? Yes. But you could have written it? No. You see, it's all assumptions based on ignorance."

"Just like I assume he's an idiot."

"Well, not really. Your assumption has a basis in fact. His is based on stereotypes. I mean, black kids from the slums steal, right? So how big a stretch is it for him to decide you stole the writing and passed it off as your own? This is the thinking you're up against. It's not only vicious, it's bred in the bone, I'm afraid. You know that, don't you, Jamal?"

"Oh yeah. I know it all right."

Forrester walked into the living room, making a straight line for the liquor cabinet.

"A little early for you, isn't it? It's half past four."

"Somewhere in the world it's five. Somewhere else it's six, or seven, or eight. And by the way, don't try to be my mother. It doesn't become you."

Jamal watched as he poured an extra stiff drink.

"I think you used to know him."

"You mean Crawford?" He shook his head. "No. But he thought he knew me."

"How?"

"His book."

"But I thought you said he never got it published."

"It's a long story."

"I want to hear it."

"Well, well, the new, imperious Master Wallace. He marches in, slams my refrigerator door, questions my drinking habits and demands to know about Professor Crawford."

"I'm sorry, man. This is stress time for me."

"No need to be sorry. If I were in your shoes I'd be just as upset." He took a sip of his drink; neat for a change, Jamal noticed, no ice. "There are a lot of writers out there who know the rules of writing—where to put the comma, how to spell the words. But what they don't know what to do is write. Crawford didn't get the gift . . . and he knew it."

"So what happened?"

"So he wrote a book—a study of four writers who *did* know how to write. I was the only one of them still alive. Crawford managed to convince my publisher to buy it, and the sponsoring editor, a pleasant, intelligent woman I knew rather well—she'd been the secretary to my editor when my novel was published—she let me vet the manuscript. She was concerned with libel questions, but there was more than libel to worry about. It was just plain awful. Plain stupid from top to bottom. The most banal kind of lit-psych nonsense you've ever read. I informed the editor—and followed it up with a letter to the publisher—that if I ever saw that book in print they would never get a second book from me."

"And Crawford's book went away," Jamal said.

Forrester nodded and smiled. "Into thin air. There are times when clout comes in handy. This was one of those times."

"But you already knew there wasn't going to be any second book. What's up with that?"

"True. But they didn't know. And I'm not dead yet. They still may be hoping they'll get their book some day."

Jamal left Forrester's apartment early that evening, having worked through his anger with the old novelist's help. He might be getting the shaft from Crawford, but then Crawford had gotten the shaft from Forrester. It was a neat pattern of tit for tat that appealed to Jamal's sense of justice. He promised himself to stay cool in Crawford's class, continue to do his work and not give the man the satisfaction of knowing what he thought of him. *A disappointed writer is a dangerous animal,* Jamal decided.

He walked to the nearest Starbucks, where his mother worked long hours, often taking on two shifts to help pay the bills. Since transferring to Mailor-Callow, Jamal had seen very little of her and sometimes she couldn't hide the hurt when he missed a meal or was curt in conversation, eager to get back to his writing. He loved his mother more than he could express in spoken words (he wrote them, though, and one day she would read his words and they would make her proud). She had brought Jamal and his brother up alone, with no help. She despised welfare, which she considered institutionalized charity, and often worked two jobs rather than accept a handout. He had never gone without food or clothes or spending money, and most important of all, never a moment without her love and her belief in him.

He entered and spotted her immediately behind the counter, bent over the coffee machine. He watched her for a moment before approaching her. Two young white girls—Mailor-Callow types—were asking his mother, with well-bred politeness, if they could please have decaf cappuccinos, as though without her permission they would just have to slink away without a drink. Jamal looked around. All the customers were white, everyone looked well off. *Why do I like Claire so much?* he asked himself. *She's just like them—white, privileged, rich.* But, no, he knew she wasn't like them. But was he a victim of her friendliness, tricked by her seeming interest in him? His stomach lurched with a wave of nausea. Claire was confusion, pure confusion. He looked back at his mother, this frail, middle-aged black woman with what his father used to call her million dollar smile in the days before the smile evidently was not enough. Why did it have to be this way? She deserved better than to be at the beck and call of the white world for the peanuts Starbucks paid her. Maybe he should perfect his game and hit the pros right out of high school—forget about college, forget about writing. He had a responsibility to his mother. He closed his eyes and swept a hand across his forehead, then pressed his temples. He felt a bad one coming on.

"Hi, Ma." He forced a smile.

"Hey, Jamal. Lose your keys again?"

"No. They're in my backpack."

"I'm sure. Along with the subway pass you forgot to take today."

"Hey, no one's perfect. I just figured you might like a walk home."

Her smile shifted to a true warmth, a soft glow in the eyes, the kind of smile the Starbucks patrons never saw. "I would like that. Just let me finish up."

They drifted slowly south toward home, in easy conversation, although Jamal skirted any discussion of Professor Crawford. His mother had enough worries without that. Mrs. Wallace touched the sleeve of his jacket and said, "This isn't for winter. We have to get you an overcoat."

"I don't like heavy things, Ma," he answered with a touch of annoyance. "How many times do I have to tell you that?"

"I suppose you're gonna tell me you're not cold."

"I'm not."

She sighed. After a block of silence, she said, "Your light's been on late."

"Don't worry about me."

"It's my job to worry about you." She paused, choosing her words carefully. "Like when I call home to check on you at night . . . and you aren't there. Which has been happening too much lately."

"There's been a lot goin' on at school."

"At eleven at night?"

"There's this professor I work with. He thinks I'm good and he helps me with my writing."

Mrs. Wallace took his hand, but as there were people in the street he quickly pulled it away. "So things are all right with you?"

"Yeah . . . They're all right. Just different."

With an anxious smile, she said, "Good different?"

"It's like I'm tryin' and all . . . but . . . I don't know—if you don't belong there you might need more than effort."

141

"Are you really trying, Jamal? That's a new approach for you. You're so quick you've always skated through everything. It comes so easy for you."

"It's different now. The work demands real concentration—and then I come back here . . . and my friends . . . well it's different. Everything's changed."

"It's different for them, too, not having you around so much. They'll figure it out."

Jamal gave her a sidelong glance, judging her reaction, as he said, "Maybe kids from the Bronx belong in the Bronx."

"Don't start up with me now, Jamal Wallace. Feeling sorry for yourself is no answer, and you're not too old to take over my knee. Kids belong where they belong. Just remember one thing—God gave you a great gift and it can take you anywhere you want to go."

Jamal grinned. "You just try taking me over your knee."

"Don't vex me now," she said with an answering smile.

She unlocked the door and they entered the apartment, which smelled clean and inviting, thanks to her incessant cleaning and scrubbing. Jamal immediately headed toward his room, then stopped.

"Ma—you've spent a lot on me since I started Mailor. You'd let me know if we didn't, you know, if it was all getting to be too much. I can get a job at the Key baggin' groceries. The night shift."

Mrs. Wallalce leafed through a stack of mail, some with the bill windows clearly visible, before looking up. "There's enough worries in the world to divide between us. You can't shoulder them all. You take school, I'll handle the rest. Okay?"

"If you say so. But you gotta let me know if it gets too much."

She glanced left and right as though looking for someone. "Are we alone?"

"Huh?"

"Yes, we're alone." She put her arms around her son and held him close. "Nobody to embarrass you now."

"Ma, you know something? You're the mushiest woman in the world."

He hugged her back.

Chapter 14

Having to write under Professor Crawford's watchful eye was proving to be a disaster. Jamal was keenly aware of the man's presence, his probing eye, and he couldn't make the leap from Crawford and the classroom setting to the creative world where ideas formed and linked and the words flowed as though written by an automatic hand. He could hear the rustling of the professor's *New York Times* as he turned the pages. He could hear the man's breathing and the constant clearing of his throat. Every time he looked up, the man seemed to be staring at him, his eyes cold and appraising, taking his measure. Jamal had always loved to write, and had never experienced writer's block, but now he knew the torture of looking at a blank page and not having the slightest idea what to fill it with. The blank page mocked him. The man's presence was killing his desire to write.

At the end of his first session with Crawford, the professor folded his newspaper, rose from behind his desk and stuck it in his briefcase, which he then snapped closed.

"Mr. Wallace?"

Jamal refused to look at him.

"I'm addressing you, sir." He reached for Jamal's paper, glanced at it, and a brief smile crossed his face. "I hate to think this is a case of Johnny in *The Shining*," he said with a hint of amusement.

"I can't write under these conditions." Jamal continued to stare at his desk.

"Well, give some thought to trying again tomorrow."

Jamal watched Crawford walk out of the room with his paper, on which, the sum of his hour's work, was his signature and date on the top right.

"This game has got to stop," he muttered, picking up his pencil and breaking it in half.

The next morning, Professor Crawford was scribbling on the blackboard as the students trickled into class. Jamal took a seat without looking at the front of the room. He had stayed up most of the night putting the finishing touches on his competition entry. It had taken him more than an hour to get in the flow, still caught up in the anger and frustration of his session with Crawford, but finally words and images and fresh ideas filled his mind and drowned out all other thoughts.

A few students walked to the front and placed folders on the professor's desk. With his eyes still on the blackboard, Crawford said, "It sounds like the rich tradition of handing in competition entries on the final day"—he stopped writing and wiped chalk from his hands with a tissue—"continues for another year."

As he turned, he saw, with a flicker of surprise, that Jamal was standing at his desk dropping a paper in his wire mesh basket. The two locked expressions for a moment before Jamal returned to his seat.

There was a buzzing in the room, the nervous energy of the start of a new school day, before Crawford raised a hand and said, "People . . . if you don't mind."

Claire dashed in late and took the first empty seat she could find in the back, rather than risk attracting the professor's attention.

Crawford turned to the words he had written on the board. He began to recite in sonorous tones: "'Ere sin could blight or sorrow fade, death comes with friendly care. The opening bud to Heaven convey'd, and bade it blossom there.'"

He did a little stiff swivel and peered over the top of his glasses at the class.

"Anyone?"

No one spoke.

"A little more morning reticence than usual, I see."

Crawford glanced back at the words and read them again very slowly and with exaggerated emphasis, the way some people speak singsong English to foreigners in the hope that the words will suddenly make sense to the slow and stupid.

"Mr. Coleridge," he said to the long-haired blonde youth who had become friendly with Jamal and occasionally joined him and Claire for lunch.

Coleridge lowered his body a few inches deeper in his chair.

Professor Crawford motioned for him to stand. "Mr. Coleridge, how many students would you say we have in my lecture class today?"

The boy looked around blankly and shrugged. "I'm not sure. You want me to count?"

There was a titter in the room, which Crawford stopped dead with a scowl and a chopping motion. "Maybe you could humor us with a guess."

"Forty?"

"Not a bad guess, Mr. Coleridge. Let's assume forty. Now of the forty bodies temporarily in residence here, apparently there isn't one that knows the author of this passage. I find that remarkable. Don't you find that remarkable, Mr. Coleridge?"

The boy shook his head timidly in the affirmative, not trusting himself to speak.

Crawford strolled to the blackboard again. He said, "Perhaps we should back into this a bit. Mr. Coleridge, in looking at this passage, what, if any, conclusions might we be able to draw?"

The boy's fingers fluttered to his mouth in panic. Coleridge was a passionate and reasonably talented guitar player of the blues and funk persuasion, who at the moment wanted nothing more than to hit the open road with his instrument and never return to Manhattan and school.

"You—you mean about the author?" he stuttered.

"About anything."

Coleridge stared at him, mouth slightly ajar.

"Come, come," said the professor. "Do any of the words strike you as . . . unusual?"

The boy breathed in deeply and said, "Ere?"

"Ere. Yes. And why is that an unusual word?"

"Because it sounds old. I never heard anybody use it."

"Yes, it does sound old. And do you know *why* it sounds old, Mr. Coleridge?"

The boy blinked, opened his mouth but said nothing.

"It's because it *is* old. Almost two hundred years old. This passage was written before you were born, before your father was born, before your father's father's father was born." Crawford walked closer to Coleridge, who shrank back and seemed to fold in on himself. "But that still does not excuse the fact that *you* don't know who wrote the poem of which this passage is a part. Now does it, Mr. Coleridge?"

"I'm . . . sorry . . . Sir. I—"

"You, of all the people in the room—you should know who wrote these words—and do you know why you should know, Mr. Coleridge? Do you have even the tiniest clue as to why?"

Jamal leaned forward from two rows behind Coleridge and whispered, "Just say your name, man."

Crawford's glanced pierced Jamal. "I'm sorry, I didn't hear you. Do you have something to contribute, Mr. Wallace? I'm sure we'd all like to know what it is."

"I said he should say his name."

"And why would it be helpful for Mr. Coleridge to say his name?

"Because that's who wrote the poem."

A hush enveloped the room. The slightest sound of in-drawn breath was the only sound. Everyone watched with the fascination of spectators at the scene of an accident to see how Crawford would react.

After a moment's silence, he returned to the blackboard and wrote beneath the passage: *Samuel Taylor Coleridge.* He then did a mock bow in Jamal's direction. "Very good, Mr. Wallace. Perhaps your skills do extend a bit farther than the basketball court."

Crawford strolled to the lectern and said, "Now if we can turn to page one-oh-one," as Coleridge, humiliated and pink in the face, slumped into his seat.

Jamal rose and faced Crawford.

"Yes, Mr. Wallace? Do you have something more to share with us?"

"Further," he said.

"Excuse me?"

Claire half rose and motioned to Jamal. "Don't . . ."

"The word is 'further.' You said my skills might extend farther than the basketball court."

"Yes?"

"That's incorrect, Professor Crawford. 'Farther' relates to distance. 'Further' is a definition of degree." The other students had drawn one collective breath and were stone silent. "You should have said 'further.'"

Crawford's cheeks quivered and his voice was a few notes higher as he said, "Are you challenging me, Mr. Wallace? And in my own classroom?"

Jamal hesitated for an instant, then plunged on. "Not any more than you challenged John. Maybe less. I was just pointing out a wrong usage."

Crawford studied Jamal with partly closed eyes as though he were seeing him for the first time. "Perhaps the challenge," he said, "should have been directed elsewhere."

"I'm not sure I follow you, Professor Crawford."

"I think you do."

Jamal continued to stand, continued to lock gazes with Crawford.

"All right, Mr. Wallace, let's see what you know." He went to the blackboard, started to write, then dropped the chalk and turned to Jamal.

"'It is a melancholy truth that even——'"

"'——that even great men have poor relations.' Dickens."

The class began to murmur until Crawford raised a hand and shouted harshly, "Quiet, please." He glared at Jamal. "'You will hear the beat of a horse's feet and the swish of a——'"

"Kipling," Jamal finished.

"'All great truths begin as——'"

"Shaw," Jamal said.

Crawford clenched his fists. "'Man is the only animal that——'"

"'——blushes.' Mark Twain." Jamal spread his arms and shrugged. "C'mon, man, is that the best you can do to humiliate me?"

Crawford slammed a fist on the side of the lectern; it wobbled and nearly fell. "Get out, Wallace. *Get out.*"

"Sure, I'd be glad to." Jamal gathered his books. "I've got better things to do with my time."

He swung open the door and was halfway out, about to slam the door behind him, when Claire squeezed through before it closed.

"Jamal . . ."

"Leave it alone, Claire. This is my fight."

"Just hold on . . . please. He's a complete idiot, but he's got the power."

"Is this the way things work around here? They throw you out of class if you know something—and if you don't know something they ridicule you? Is this what goes down? Because if it is, I'm outta here. He's just a dumb, pretentious fool."

"You have no idea what he can do to students who stand up to him—really challenge him. It isn't pretty."

"You know something, Claire? Right now I don't care in the slightest."

The following day, a Saturday, Jamal went to Forrester's early and recounted the entire incident while the old writer was washing a stack of yesterday's dishes.

"'Further' and 'farther,'" Forrester said with a snort of laughter. "What a clod the man is. A pedant like him should do better."

"I annoyed him big time. I'm in trouble."

"You think you should apologize?"

"No." He looked at his friend carefully. "Are you thinking I should?"

"You beat him at his own game," Forrester replied. "Nothing to be sorry about." He paused to squirt more soap on his sponge. "It's a good thing, though, to be careful."

"What's that mean?"

"What it means is, don't let yourself be sidetracked by others' mediocrity. Or their envy. You've been blessed with a gift that will allow you to do some remarkable things in life, years from now." He looked up from his dishwashing. "That is, if you don't screw up by being a sixteen year old right now."

Chapter 15

The Mailor-Callow basketball team had compiled an unbeaten record as their season came down to the three final games. In their division, Jamal was second in total points scored, averaging twenty-five a game, first in assists with six-point-five, and he also led in steals with three a game. He knew that he had a chance to make the all-city high school starting lineup as either a point or a shooting guard, but he gave little thought to that. At the not-so-subtle suggestion of Coach Garrick, he was in the process of trying to change his game. Garrick had called him into his office after a recent practice session, put his feet on his desk and said, with no preliminaries, "Jamal, you've got a big talent. You know that, right?"

"It's nice to hear, Coach."

"You're leading the world in practically every category—but you know something? I'm not satisfied."

Jamal looked at him in surprise. "You're not?" Garrick had an abrasive personality, but Jamal respected him for his shrewd, minute-by-minute tactical grasp of the game and for his democratic treatment of his players: He never overtly favored one over another. "What am I doin' wrong?"

"Nothing," Garrick replied. "You hustle, you deliver. It's just that I want you to do certain right things more than some other right things." He put his feet down and leaned across the desk. "Do you see yourself as a one or two guard?"

Jamal grinned. "Well, Coach, I guess I blur the distinctions."

"Right on. Good players have a way of doing that. Take Hartwell now—he's an example of a fine talent who's fit for one position."

Jamal nodded. "Two guard."

"You got it. The boy can put the ball in the hoop."

"So can I," said Jamal, shifting nervously from foot to foot.

Garrick waved the comment off impatiently. "We know that, but that's not the issue here. I want you to take over the game at point from here on through the state tournament. Distribute the ball, involve everyone—make everyone happy. They touch the ball—and I'm including Hartwell. Most of all Hartwell. And you know why? No offense, but he's a natural shooter, just like you."

"Maybe he's a more natural shooter."

"Maybe. The thing is, let him score. I want your assists in the ten to twelve range. Are you okay with that?"

"Yeah. I'm the conductor."

Garrick slapped the table and grinned. "You've got it, Jamal. Lead these guys. You're the only one who can do it."

The next practice session went more smoothly than any since Jamal had joined the team. He took every opportunity to find and feed Hartwell; he worked on using his foot speed to penetrate and then kick out to the open man, setting screens and picks. Garrick was right; they were an even better team when Jamal orchestrated and involved the other players, and as an added plus, there was less friction between him and Hartwell. Reluctantly he also had to admit that coach was right about Hartwell: The arrogant guy had a sweet shot, every bit as sweet as his.

A pep rally was held after the final game of the regular schedule. The Mailor-Callow students were packed in the gym shoulder to shoulder. Coach Garrick stood at a center-court microphone, his face flushed with emotion. He shouted into it: "This is the best team I've coached in my eleven years here. These boys play hard, scramble for the loose balls, and execute intelligently." He paused before the punch line. "They even listen to me." That line brought wild laughter from the students; the players, listening in the locker room, grinned and glanced at one another. Coach was not known for his wit.

"Friday night," Garrick continued, "this team will start its run at a state championship. It will bring something into Madison Square Garden that no other team can claim this year." The cheering grew louder. "And that's a record of twenty-three wins and no losses." The last words were lost in a wild crescendo of noise. "Remember—this is *your* team . . . and they're counting on *your* support this weekend. . . ."

The players huddled in the locker room, waiting to be called out, were pumped. They were ready to start the tournament right now, tonight. Hartwell and Jamal stood at opposite ends of the room, still caught up in their season-long chill off court, although during games the two boys had become a finely meshed machine.

The players heard Coach Garrick say, "Would you please help me welcome the top-ranked high school team in the state of New York!"

Hartwell, looking everywhere but at Jamal, yelled out, "All right, men, let's get out there. . . ."

He led the team onto the court, but Jamal leaned against the wall for an extra second before heading out. Claire, in the front of the crowd, jumping up and down, gave him a slow wink and a thumbs-up gesture. He grinned, then quickly looked away.

When the rally was over, Jamal walked past Garrick's office and stopped when the coach called out to him. "Hey, Wallace."

"Yes, Coach?"

"We get an hour to practice in the Garden tomorrow." He grinned, still red faced and sweating from the pep rally. "You interested?"

"Are you kidding? That's been my dream forever."

"Bus leaves right after school. I know you and time aren't always on the best of terms."

"Ah, Coach, that's just a rumor. I'll be the first one on board."

Garrick reached for a message on his scattered desk. "Oh . . . you got a call from the office. They want to see you in the conference room."

Jamal took the message and stared at it. "Now? It's almost five o'clock."

Garrick shrugged. "You better hurry over there. Just don't miss the bus tomorrow, okay?"

Jamal forced himself to walk slowly; he made a conscious effort to gather himself and remain calm. His antennae were operating again and they told him that something was wrong, and they also warned him that Professor Crawford was there at the center of it.

He cautiously entered the Mailor-Callow conference room, a long, polished mahogany table splitting the room in two. The table, the claw-foot chairs, the nineteenth century landscape paintings on the walls and the three men sitting at the table, suggested a meeting of *Fortune 500* honchos rather than a high school conference involving an eleventh grade student. At the far end of the room staring at him as he entered were Professor Crawford, Professor Matthews, and Dr. George Spence, Claire's father.

What's going on here? This is bad news, man. This sucks.

Jamal stood at the table returning their stares, struggling to retain his composure and show nothing.

Crawford motioned toward a nearby chair. "Please take a seat, Mr. Wallace."

Without a word he took a seat and laced both of his hands on the table to keep them steady.

"I believe you know both of these gentlemen. Professor Matthews of the faculty board . . . and Dr. Spence, a member of the board of trustees."

"Jamal," they both said at once.

154

He nodded in acknowledgement but remained silent. *Let the fox make the first move. The rabbit will respond.*

Crawford shuffled through a stack of papers in front of him.

"The three of us," he began slowly, "have been reviewing some of the work submitted for this year's writing competition. . . and we were hoping you might clarify a couple of points concerning your submission." He peered at Jamal over the top of his glasses and there was not a hint of friendship in his gaze. He pushed a stapled paper in front of Jamal. "'A Season of Faith's Perfection.' Your piece, correct?"

Jamal took a quick glance. "Yes. That's mine."

Crawford cleared his throat, a hand to his mouth, and regarded Jamal thoughtfully. "Mr. Wallace, it's standard policy for us to ask our students if they wish to credit any source material, or"—a polite cough—"if they wish to, ah, credit a co-author when turning in an assignment of this magnitude." He paused and Jamal was aware that all three men were staring at him intently, waiting for his answer.

He hesitated for an instant, sensing a trap, but having no idea what the trap could possibly be. Finally, with a shake of his head, he said, "No. It's my work."

The professor's eyes glowed with an expression Jamal interpreted as triumph. He was on his guard, but what good would it do when he was guarding against the unknowable? Three sets of eyes bore into him.

Crawford said, "So you wish to take sole credit as the author of this essay?"

Jamal nodded.

"Are you saying it's entirely your work?" Dr. Spence asked.

"Yes, sir."

Without a word, Crawford slipped a second set of papers across the desk. When he stared at the top page Jamal felt a stab of pain in his temples so strong that he wanted to grab his head and squeeze it. It took all of his will to keep his expression neutral.

"'A Season of Faith's Perfection,' Mr. Wallace. "Is that the title?"

"Yes."

"An essay from nineteen fifty-nine, published by *The New Yorker* magazine." Crawford paused, heaving a heavy sigh, and said, "The author of the piece is William Forrester."

You lied to me. You let me believe there was only the novel, a lie by omission, and you encouraged me to go down that road, and the road ends with a sign that says, So long, Jamal. You're toast, man.

Jamal stared numbly at the essay. The unknowable was now on the table and there were no words to cover this. The very worst—this work of Forrester's—lay under his hand.

Crawford went on in a soft, sepulchral voice. "The majority of the piece is actually quite original in content, aside from an occasional sentence here and there. And then, of course, there is the title to consider."

Jamal looked up from the paper into Professor Crawford's eyes, but still said nothing.

Matthews said, "Jamal, this is a serious accusation. I assume you know that."

"I know." He started to say more, but there was no way he could say more without involving Forrester, and he would never reveal their secret; he would die first.

Crawford said, "Mr. Wallace, I'm afraid that as of this morning your entry is withdrawn. And, following school policy, you have to be placed on immediate probation pending a review by the board. Next week."

Jamal looked from one man to the next, his mouth open with shock. All their expressions were set, steely, unsympathetic. "Probation?"

When Dr. Spence spoke, his words were more conciliatory than his stony gaze. He said, "Jamal . . . the timing of all this is unfortunate, considering the events of this coming weekend." He tried a smile. "I understand that without you in the lineup we're no more than a pretty good team—certainly not a great one. So . . . we'd like to offer a solution that we feel is in everyone's best interests." He turned to Professor Crawford. "Robert?"

"Yes. Well obviously, the most important thing is making quite certain this type of violation doesn't repeat itself." He squinted at Jamal and his voice dropped in volume and temperature as he said, "Therefore you'll be required to write a letter of apology to your fellow students, the ones you took advantage of by submitting this paper. Also, you'll be required to read that letter in front of my class."

The three men waited for Jamal to respond. He said finally, "Are you serious with this?"

"These are our terms, Mr. Wallace."

"But that's crazy, man. It's just crazy."

"You have no other option, I'm afraid. You can be placed on probation as of this minute and miss this weekend's tournament—and risk being expelled from this school. Your choice."

Jamal stared grimly at Crawford, but said nothing more.

Dr. Spence stood and turned to Jamal.

He likes the angle. Towering over me.

He said, "You haven't given us many choices here, you know. You are obviously an intelligent young man, and I hope you make an intelligent decision. We'll need that letter written before next week's board meeting. Is that understood?"

"Yes."

Dr. Spence nodded at Crawford and walked toward the door; Matthews gathered his papers and followed.

When they had left the room, Crawford leaned across the conference table and whispered, "One last word, Wallace. Don't ever embarrass me in front of my class again."

Jamal stood at the front entrance to Mailor-Callow, figuring that Claire hadn't gone directly home from the pep rally (the rally seemed like an event from another lifetime), but was waiting to ride to Long Island with her father. Waiting, maybe, to talk to him.

He was about to leave when she walked up. She didn't hug him but stood at a distance, and her expression was solemn.

"Hello, Jamal."

"Have you talked to your father yet?"

"He's waiting for me. I said I had to speak to you."

"I didn't get my essay from *The New Yorker* piece."

"Please, Jamal. Give me some credit."

"I'm telling the truth."

"Oh—so the words 'A Season of Faith's Perfection' just happened to pop into your head. Is that what you're asking me to believe?"

"I'm not asking you for anything," he said, an edge in his voice.

Her eyes were red and swollen, on the verge of tears. "I'm so disappointed. I don't know what to say." She looked everywhere but into his eyes. "Those papers you tucked into the copy of *Avalon Landing* you gave me? What you wrote was so. . . God, it was so wonderful and I loved it that you knew how good you were. You just *knew*, and didn't try to hide or pretend." Her voice began to unravel as the tears came. "It seemed to matter so much. That's what I loved."

She waited for a response, something, anything to make it all right, but he regarded her with no expression.

She shrugged and moved toward the waiting town car.

"Claire?"

She turned.

"It was Forrester."

"I knew it was Forrester."

"No." He pressed his temples, pressed against the searing pain. "He read a couple of my things and—well, he pledged me to secrecy. You're the only one . . . I haven't told anyone but you. But . . . he's been reading all my stuff. I see him every day. He's teaching me."

Claire continued to cry but there was also a glint of anger in her eyes. "Do you expect me to believe that? *No one* talks to William Forrester. How did I ever come to trust you, Jamal? I would've trusted you with my life. Now I just feel sick."

Chapter 16

Jamal traveled home in a fog, hardly aware that he was riding the subway. He sat with his backpack on his lap, staring ahead at nothing. Claire now hated him, Forrester had deceived him, and the school might toss him out. *I wish I knew how to cry,* he thought. But the last time he had cried was when he was eleven years old and his father left the family. After that, there were no tears left to cry.

He went directly to Forrester's apartment and knocked on the door. The old writer slid open the peephole and saw Jamal bent forward under the weight of his backpack. He opened the door.

"Where's your key?"

Jamal walked by him without a word.

"I see we're passing on the conventional greetings today."

Jamal dropped his backpack on the table and turned to face Forrester.

"About the key, I didn't want to use it."

"And why is that?"

"Having a key to your place is an intimate thing."

"So?"

"William, how come you told me to write something you'd already published? I mean, *why?*" Forrester clenched his jaws. "Be careful where you take this."

With a violent shake of his head, Jamal opened his backpack and pulled out his essay. He thrust it at Forrester.

"The piece we worked on together—the one you told me you liked so much—'Great work, Jamal'—'You're going places, Jamal'. . . . Why didn't you tell me you sold it to a magazine?"

"Why should it matter?" Forrester said, raising his voice. His chest was puffed out and he was breathing fast.

"It matters," Jamal said, his voice also rising.

"The object of a question," said Forrester, "is to obtain information that matters to us. Why should this matter to you?" He studied Jamal closely, his expression dark. "Or does it matter to someone else?"

They locked glances.

"What did you do with it, Jamal?"

"You should have told me."

"What did you *do* with it?"

"I thought *Avalon Landing* was the only writing you ever published. You led me to believe that."

Forrester slammed his fist on the table. "It doesn't matter what you believed. What did you do with it?"

Jamal stepped forward until they were no more than a foot apart. "I turned it in," he said. He looked away from the heat in Forrester's eyes. "I had to show Crawford something."

"You promised me that anything we wrote in here—"

"I know, I *know*—"

"—would *stay* in here. We talked about that, didn't we? We agreed to that."

"I know!"

"No, you *don't* know—you don't know anything. Why didn't you listen?"

"I thought—I don't know, I did all this work . . . and . . . I messed up, didn't I?" He felt tears press against his forehead, a flood of tears, but he held them back. *Don't cry, man. Don't ever do that. You can't let him know how you feel.*

After a moment's silence, Forrester said, "Are you in trouble over this?"

Jamal nodded. "Yeah. Big time trouble."

"What are they telling you?"

161

"I go on probation unless I write a letter sayin' I was wrong. Apologizing to my classmates. Then I have to stand up in front of them and read it out loud."

"Write the letter."

"I'm not writin' anything, man."

"You got Crawford, now he gets you. Write the letter. The only thing he can do is humiliate you."

"And you'd let him do that?"

"You created the problem, remember." Forrester turned his back on Jamal, scooping ice into a glass at the liquor cabinet.

"I didn't plagiarize from your work."

"I know that."

"Yeah, but *they* don't."

"You see what you got yourself into? You have to learn to clean up your own messes."

"You know something, William? I'm sick and tired of everything being some kind of life lesson. You want to know what the lesson is here? It's that the title of *your* essay is at the top of my paper. That's your lesson, man."

"I wasn't the one who turned it in."

"No. You were just the one who got me involved in all this. When, Jesus, all you had to tell me was, 'Hey, Jamal, don't let this out of the apartment because I sold it to *The New Yorker* forty years ago.'"

"I told you to keep everything here. That was our bargain. You broke it."

Forrester poured his drink and took a long swallow.

Now is the moment. Fish or cut bait time now. Say it, man— say it.

"William—I could use a little help on this one."

Forrester shook his head. "I'm afraid that's not an option."

"You don't have to go anywhere or see anyone. Just write a letter to Crawford explaining the situation."

"I said—I repeat—that is not an option."

Jamal nodded, trying to hide his disappointment. "Okay, man, if you don't want to help me, that's cool. It's no big thing. I've got a nice little history of people not helping me."

"Oh, Christ," Forrester said with a snort of derision, "not this self-pity father nonsense. It doesn't become you."

Jamal squeezed his eyes shut against the swelling migrane worming its way into his brain. "What did you say?"

"You heard me. You just didn't stick to the bargain. I had my reasons for insisting on it."

Reaching for the strap of his backpack, Jamal said, "Yeah. . . well, that's okay, man. You interested in some reasons that have nothing to do with self-pity or my father? How about you letting me take it on this one because you're too scared to walk out that door and maybe do something for someone else. Try that for a reason."

"Don't you tell me about reasons," Forrester said, slamming his drink down on the table, spilling half of it. "You don't know one thing about reasons." He advanced on Jamal as though he might attack him, but Jamal stood his ground. "There are reasons for everything. Reasons why some of us are given gifts in life . . . while others are left to wonder what it feels like." He paused for breath; his forehead was bathed in sweat, although the room was cold. "And what you don't know is that there is *no reason* for that. You have decades to figure that out . . . while some . . . Oh, forget it!"

He stopped, his hands shaking, and turned his back on the conversation.

Jamal picked up his backpack and slung it over his shoulder. He said, "And what's the reason for having your desk and closet full of writing and keeping them locked up so nobody ever reads any of it? Because I still haven't figured out a good reason for doing that." He pulled out the key to Forrester's apartment and bounced it in his hand as he stared at the older man. "I'm done with it."

163

"Done with what?"

"This writing business. I've got better ways to spend my time. Maybe I've got the talent to play pro ball and make my millions."

"Is that how you feel?"

"Yes."

"Then get out. *Get out.*"

Jamal tossed him the key, but he made no effort to catch it.

"The only reason I let you in that door was because of your writing." His hand shook as he picked up his glass. "If you're done . . . so are we."

Jamal stood in the doorway and looked back. "That's all right, man. You've been done for forty years."

That night, Jamal broke down and cried in his mother's arms. She called in sick and sat with him on his bed while he talked on and on—about his rage against his father, about his writing, about his feelings for Claire Spence, his problems with Professor Crawford—and about William Forrester. She rubbed his back and shoulders and listened carefully, and she didn't say a word until he was finished. He wiped his eyes with his knuckles.

"God, what a wuss," he said. "Maybe I should be wearing a dress."

"Men cry, too, honey. There's nothing wrong with it."

"It's weak." She smiled and punched his arm softly. "You carry grief too long inside it can poison you. Your tears are medicine—you need them sometimes. I've watched you over the years, trying to be strong and steady—but you'll learn that real weakness is when you can't admit to weakness."

Jamal tried to smile. "Ma, that's deep. Where'd you pick up that theory?"

"Forty-five years of living. The best reality school there is." She studied his face with concern. "Migraine?"

"Yeah."

"You seein' those auras?"

"Not that bad."

She began to massage the top of his head, working slowly down behind his ears. "Who else knows about William Forrester?"

"Terrell. He took us to Yankee Stadium one night. I told Claire. But she doesn't believe me."

Mrs. Wallace nodded. "Baby, this isn't an easy one to believe."

"I know. It hurts, though, her thinking I'm a liar."

"I'm not about to tell you what to do here," she said slowly, "because I don't know the answer. But I do know that when it comes to getting in schools like this one—I mean, how many chances will we have? People like us don't get these kind of breaks, not in this neighborhood they don't." She searched his face. "Am I right?"

"You're right."

"And if it means doing somethin' you might not want to do?"

"That's the problem."

"I know. And I can't solve it for you. You've got to make this decision on your own. It's a man's decision."

"Yeah." He closed his eyes, feeling the pain recede under his mother's hands. "You know what's the worst part?"

"What?"

"It's the first time I really believed in myself . . . and I got nobody believing in me."

She kissed the top of his head. "I believe in you."

"Thanks, Ma."

"Jamal?"

"Yeah?"

"You still believe in yourself, don't you?"

"That's the trouble," he said. "I don't know."

Chapter 17

Ever since he was a small boy Jamal had dreamed that one day he would play ball in Madison Square Garden in front of nineteen thousand screaming fans. In the dream he wore the Knicks uniform and his joy knew no bounds as he cut through the lane, lost his man, soared, swished. The dream was now reality; he and his Mailor-Callow teammates were practicing for the first game of the state tournament on Friday night. But it was far from the reality he had envisioned for so many years. Instead of joy, his heart was full of bitterness. In exchange for this chance to play and help honor the school with a championship, he was being forced to sacrifice his own honor. He was sadly aware that by standing on this court of his dreams he was giving in to Crawford and everything he hated.

As he sprinted up and down the court, he tried to drive the dark thoughts from his mind. He picked a pass out of the air and lightly laid it into the basket.

"All right," screamed Coach Garrick. "Shoot your free throws and we're outta here."

Jamal took the ball and moved to the line in his familiar slouch, head hung slightly forward. He stood at the line, dribbled the ball a number of times, and as he looked at the rim a kind of haze settled over his mind. He was in the Garden, but he was also in Forrester's apartment. For just an instant he couldn't separate illusion from reality.

Hartwell, standing behind Jamal, shouted, "Any time, Wallace. Meditate later, man."

Jamal snapped out of it, dribbled again and calmly made the free throw.

Coach Garrick called him over and slung an arm around his shoulder. "You okay?"

"Yeah."

"You're just a fraction slow on everything today. You got to pick it up."

"I'll be okay."

"You sure?"

Jamal nodded.

"We're depending on you," Garrick said. "I don't want this thing with the board messin' your head up tomorrow night." He lowered his voice. "You're my main man, you know that." He clapped Jamal on the back. "We cool on that?"

"We're cool, Coach."

Garrick put a hand to his mouth, megaphone style, and yelled, "All right, men, let's wrap it up!"

Toward evening, as the late winter sun was beginning to fade, Jamal wandered through his neighborhood. It felt strange to be at loose ends—no homework, no writing he wanted to do . . . no Forrester. He studied the buildings, the streets, the people as though he was seeing everything for the first time. He knew that he had changed and that he no longer fitted in. He had become a stranger in this world he had known all his life. But if not here, where did he fit in? Had he cut himself adrift with no safe harbor in sight? Forrester was gone, Claire was gone. What was there that he could claim for his own?

As though in search of an answer, he drifted by Franklin High where a spirited pickup game was in progress on the cracked and broken concrete. He stood in the shadows and watched without being seen. He forced himself not to look at Forrester's window. His old friends were playing—Fly, Kenzo, Damon and the rest—and, like the neighborhood, they were both the same and not the same. It had all changed for him in a matter of a few short months. The trash talking, strutting, daredevil joy they brought to the game he had owned only six months earlier, but now he played a different game—maybe a better one, but it was more of a white man's game.

He approached the court and the players finally noticed him. Fly grabbed the ball, stopped the game and said, indifferently, "Hey, Jamal Wallace." Damon nodded to him and Kenzo said, "Hey, man. What's up? You ain't been around."

"Same old stuff," Jamal said. "School's keepin' me busy." He looked at Fly. "You got a spot?"

"Court's full," Fly answered.

There was an awkward silence, which Jamal finally broke, saying, "Yeah, cool. I'll just watch for a while."

"Later, man," Damon said.

Fly nodded at him but said nothing. He threw the ball in and the game continued. Jamal leaned against the school wall and watched for a few minutes, but he felt uncomfortable as a spectator, and besides, the game struck him as crude—all flair and no finesse. After a Fly jam, he slipped away for the walk home.

The following night, twenty minutes before game time, the Mailor-Callow players gathered around Coach Garrick in the locker room; his face was redder than usual and his brown eyes bulged with emotion. The players could hear the Mailor band blaring oncourt and students chanting and yelling—"Mailor go . . . Mailor *go* . . ." mixed with the chants and screams of the Columbia Prep followers.

The P-A announcer cut in over the general hubbub: "New York's Madison Square Garden, the world's most famous sports arena, welcomes you to tonight's opening round of the New York State High School Basketball Championship."

Garrick was strolling back and forth, chewing furiously on a wad of gum.

"I need thirty-two minutes out of everyone of you tonight. Not twenty, not twenty-eight—thirty-two! Treat them like the most important thirty-two minutes of your life, because that's how long you'll remember them."

Jamal stared at the floor, at his tight double-laced sneakers. He didn't want to think. *Just play, man, get lost in the action. They'll be time for thinking later. Right now get through it, give yourself to the game. . . .*

Hartwell gathered the players together at the tunnel exit, their heads bowed toward the center of the circle.

"All right, this is it. We haven't lost one yet and we're not gonna start tonight. We go at these guys and we don't let up." He put his hand in the center of the circle. "Everybody in," he yelled, and the other hands joined his. "On three—one, two, *three!*"

"Mailor . . . *Go!*" they yelled in unison.

They ran out onto the court (the names running through Jamal's mind—Frazier, Monroe, Bradley, Ewing, Reed, Sprewell) into a solid wall of sound, kids screaming, the band blaring. This magic moment that had played out in his fantasies for so many years was now fact: his sneakers on the same floor where the brilliant Frazier had moved with deceptive speed as he stripped opposing players with cool aplomb and made pinpoint passes and popped soft fifteen footers. *You're here, man, you're actually here!* His spirits were temporarily buoyed by the enthusiasm that had the Garden rocking, but as he began to warm up, reaching for his inner core of energy, the intensity and enthusiasm he had always depended on eluded him. He sensed it in his teammates and he worked to pump himself up mentally, but that edge he needed to give his best just wasn't there. Too many worries. Too much stuff to deal with. *C'mon, man, put it behind you. This is all there is. Tonight is the world and nothing else matters. Get down with it. Blood and sweat, man. Blood and sweat. You gotta die out here. . . .*

But it was draining out of him moment by moment; he couldn't sustain the lie. The pain behind his eyes was growing.

He took a lay up, and as he jogged back toward mid-court he spotted Crawford seated directly behind the Mailor-Callow bench. Their eyes locked, and the little smirk of triumph on the professor's face became for Jamal the dividing line between now and the rest of his life. Someone flipped him the ball; he flipped it back and started to walk slowly off the court, head down, hearing nothing, seeing nothing.

The locker room was empty. Jamal sat on the bench with his head in his hands, breathing slowly, willing his mind to blankness. Then he slowly pulled off his uniform and put on his street clothes. A shower seemed like too much effort. The Garden had become oppressive; he had to get out in the street, into the open, and walk until he couldn't walk anymore. He thought of William Forrester. He would be glued to one of his three television sets, waiting for him to perform his magic, and what a surprise the old man was in store for. *I'm not there, William. I can't ever betray you. I owe you everything, no matter what. . . .*

Coach Garrick burst into the locker room, followed by Professor Crawford, whose face looked unusually pale. Confusion and worry creased his face.

"What is going on, Wallace?" Garrick screamed. Spittle had gathered in the corners of his mouth and rope like veins stood out in his throat. "Are you sick? What the devil is it?"

"Migraine, Coach," Jamal said in a whisper. "A bad one. I'm seeing auras."

"You're *what?* Jesus, Jamal, are you sure you can't play?" He began to beg. "We need you. What's this aura thing? You've got to play."

Jamal shook his head. "I fainted in here. I'll faint again." He stared at the coach, his eyes half shut. "I'm sorry."

Garrick slammed the flat of his hand against a locker. "How can this happen now," he screamed and ran out of the room, holding his hand.

Crawford stared down at him.

"I believe you're lying."

"About the migraine?"

"Yes."

"Actually I do have one, Professor, but not so bad I couldn't play." He began to lace his Timberlands.

"If you don't go out there, you're finished," Crawford said.

Jamal looked up from his shoes. "If I play tonight, all I'm ever gonna be to this school is a basketball player. For everything else . . . I'm just discredited." He picked up his duffel bag and moved to the door. "I'm not writing your letter."

"You're making a big mistake, Wallace." But the door had closed on his words.

Jamal headed north on Seventh Avenue, kicking a pebble in front of him. As he passed Forty-second Street at Times Square, a man holding a transistor radio turned to high volume stood near him: The play-by-play man announced, "Mailor down by six early and there is still no word on why the team's top scorer, Jamal Wallace, is not on the court or even on the bench. . . ."

A decision was forming in Jamal's mind as he continued walking north. At Seventy-second Street and Central Park West he entered the park and emerged at Eighty-fourth and Fifth Avenue. He continued walking north at a slow and steady pace, blind to all around him, then angled east and walked across the Willis Avenue Bridge into the Bronx, then north again, past Yankee Stadium and another two miles to the empty playground where he had played so many joyful games for so many years. There was just enough light to see by. Jamal sat on a bench and stared at the court. Then he turned and stared up at Forrester's window, where light glowed from inside the apartment. Jamal checked his watch: five to eleven. It had taken him four hours to walk home and he knew the game was long over. He wondered who had won; hoped his school had, for the sake of all his teammates; they had worked so hard to come this far.

But on the long walk home he hadn't given any thought to the game. As block flowed into block, mile into mile, he had composed a letter—more like a speech—in his head. It was all there, perfectly polished, the paragraphs and sentences and words carefully chosen. All he had to do was write it down: simple dictation from his mind to the page. He removed a notebook from his duffel bag and began to write; when he looked up another hour had passed. He was finished. He turned and looked up at Forrester's window. It was dark now. The old man was probably passed out on his recliner, drunk again. Jamal felt a sharp stab of something . . . some emotion he couldn't recognize—troubling, profound. He tried to shake off the feeling as he rose, shouldered his duffel bag and trudged slowly home.

Chapter 18

On Saturday morning, sun streaming into his window, Jamal was deep in a dream in which has brother was wrestling him to the ground. He kicked and thrashed out, but Terrell, older and more muscular, pinned him and drew his arm up behind his back in a half nelson. "Terrell, quit, man. Enough. . . ."

He opened his eyes to see his mother and Terrell staring down at him, concern in their eyes. Jamal's heart was beating fast and his body was drenched in sweat. He looked at his mother. "Hey, Ma. I thought we had an arrangement about privacy here."

"Not today." She hesitated. "Are you all right?"

"I think so. Yeah. Well—did we win?"

"Lost in overtime," Terrell answered. "Two points."

Jamal closed his eyes and rubbed them. "Too bad. I was pullin' for them."

"But not enough to play," Terrell pointed out.

Jamal nodded. "You're right about that."

"We understand what happened," Mrs. Wallace said.

"What do you mean?" Jamal was now completely awake. He pulled himself to a sitting position.

"Your notebook," she said.

"*What?*" He glanced at the table where he had left it the night before. It was no longer there. He felt a stab of fear. Once he had composed the words in his mind and committed them to paper, they were gone and he would never be able to recapture them in just the same way. "Where is it?" he said, looking around the room. "Ma, what have you done with it?"

"Last night . . . Terrell had been looking all around the neighborhood for you. He checked Fly and your other friends, and then around midnight he saw you sitting over by Richmond. He noticed you were writing and he didn't want to bother you—you seemed okay. So he came home and told me where you were. We decided to let you do whatever you had to do."

"Where is the notebook, Ma?" Jamal's voice was harsh, man-like; it was a tone she had never heard from her younger son.

"I read it," Terrell said.

"You *what?*"

"We looked in on you . . . this must have been around two, two-thirty. You were sleepin'. I mean, look, man, you skip out on the game. You disappear. For Christ's sake, you don't think we're worried? You only think of yourself—right?"

"Terrell," Mrs. Wallace cautioned.

"You read my notebook, man."

"Jamal," his mother shouted, "that's enough!"

Terrell, locked in a staring contest with his brother, said, "There's more."

"What do you mean, 'more'? Did you burn it? Did you destroy the evidence of my insanity?" Jamal lay back on the bed and closed his eyes. "Christ!"

"I took it to him," Terrell said quietly.

Mrs. Wallace unobtrusively stepped in front of Terrell as Jamal shot back up to a sitting position.

"No—you didn't do that. . . . Tell me you didn't do that."

"I had to, Jamal. They're takin' you down at that school, and it's not right. They want to squash you and then send you back here to be one of us again—but as Ma and I were saying, you ain't one of us, little brother, and maybe you never really were. And all the stuff you wrote last night—it was for him."

"That wasn't your decision to make."

"I had to."

"It wasn't for him to see." Jamal felt the tears welling up again behind his eyes, but this time he managed to contain them.

"You're wrong. Ma figured it out. Ask her."

"Did you send him over there, Ma?"

"There was no choice. The man deserves the right to see what you wrote—and you deserve it, too."

"I guess I'm just a pawn—right? Something for both of you to move around."

Terrell said, "I went over and knocked on his door. I knocked for maybe like five minutes, then I slid the notebook under his door. I was about to take off when he opened the door and had a strange kind of smile, but when he saw it was me he got all bent out of shape. He really looks lousy, Jamal. Eyes all hollow, hair a mess. I hardly recognized him from before.

"He picked up the notebook, glanced at the first page and asked me when you wrote it. I told him last night. He wanted to know if you'd asked me to deliver it and I said you knew nothin' about my bein' there. Then he thanked me—and that was it."

Jamal stared at his mother and his brother and shook his head, biting the inside of his lip.

"Both of you leave me alone," he said. "You had no right to interfere. Just get out and close the door tight."

He sank back on the pillow and pulled the blanket over his head.

Just then the telephone rang and Mrs. Wallace hurried downstairs to answer it. A moment later, she was back knocking on his door.

"It's for you," she said.

"I'm not here," he said in muffled tones.

"It's Claire Spence."

Jamal's head emerged from beneath the blanket. "Tell her I'll be there in a minute," he said.

Mrs. Wallace and Terrell left him alone in the living room. He stared at the phone warily as though it might be alive and capable of biting him. Finally he picked it up.

"I'm amazed you're talkin' to me," he said. "How'd you get my number?"

"You gave it to me, silly. Weeks ago."

"I did?" There was a strained silence, which he broke, saying, "Why are you calling me?"

"I know why you didn't play—why you couldn't."

"Oh, yeah? Maybe you know more than I do, Claire."

"I read your papers again, then I talked to Daddy and he told me about *The New Yorker* business—Forrester's only other published work. He had a copy run off microfilm, and I begged him and begged him and finally he let me read it. Then I read your piece again. And then—then it all came together. The copy of *Avalon Landing* . . . his signature. Jamal—he gave it to you."

"Yes. He wanted me to have an unusual, unexpected present to give you. He told me that's the way to impress girls."

"Oh, Jamal, I'm so sorry . . . I'm so sorry. . . ." She started to cry. "I should have trusted you."

"That's okay," he said. "It's not your fault."

"But now I understand why you couldn't play. If you did, you were being forced to tell the Mailor board everything. That meant giving up Forrester."

"I gave him up to you."

"I know—but . . . I let you down." There was a long pause. "Jamal—I understand you're not going to write a letter of apology."

"Why should I? There's nothing to apologize for."

"Good for you. Are you coming back?"

"Only six weeks to go, Claire. I'll stick it out."

"And next year?"

"I don't get the feeling they'll want me back."

"We'll see," she said in a determined voice.

"What do you mean by that?"

"If you don't come back, I don't come back."

"Come on, Claire. You don't mean that."

"I never meant anything more in my life." She gave a weak laugh. "Daddy knows how I feel, and I already have him running scared."

"The great heart surgeon afraid of you?"

"I'm his only daughter, knucklehead. You don't understand anything, do you?"

"I'm beginning to think I don't."

"Monday's the big writing symposium award. Will you sit with me?"

"Why should I go? I'm disbarred."

"Please, Jamal . . ."

"Well, I guess so. If I don't get jumped on the way to the auditorium. The school lost because of me."

"You really don't get it, do you? The school didn't deserve to win."

Chapter 19

They arranged to meet an hour before school, for breakfast, and then enter together. Claire felt that that would deflect some attention from him. But on the way to the auditorium, a group of seniors, including John Hartwell, passed by. Hartwell refused to look at him, but one of the students said, "Thanks for showin' up, man. I think we've all just learned a new definition of the word coward."

Claire took Jamal's arm. "Come on," she said.

"The guy has a right to feel that way. I would in his position."

The auditorium was rapidly filling. The ceremony was supposed to start precisely at nine o'clock, and during his year at Mailor-Callow Jamal had learned that precisely meant just that.

They took seats on the aisle and Jamal stared at the banner hanging across the stage: 110th ANNUAL MAILOR-CALLOW WRITING SYMPOSIUM.

It was mine, he thought. *I know it was mine, but they took it away from me.*

As though she could read his thoughts, Claire reached out and took his hand. She squeezed it and smiled into his eyes. He started to pull his hand away, but she held onto it.

Jamal's attention shifted to the large photograph of Forrester on the wall. Claire, following his gaze, also stared at the photograph.

"What's he like, Jamal?"

"I don't know. He's too many things to sum up in a neat way. Gruff, moody, lonely, proud, brilliant. He's got a death wish and he needed a friend."

"You."

"Yeah. For a while he needed me."

"You told him everything, didn't you? About Crawford and submitting the piece."

"He doesn't want to see me."

"Why?"

"I said I wasn't gonna write anymore."

"You scared him."

Jamal looked at her and then at their hands, fingers intertwined.

"Me? How did I scare him?"

"He wrote one book and that was it—right?"

"Yes, but what's that got to do with me?"

"He wanted you to do what he didn't . . . or couldn't do. You're like his son, Jamal. He's passing his ambition on to you."

Jamal grinned. "Either you're brilliant or a maniac. I haven't decided which."

"Try the former."

Again Jamal gently tried to remove his hand from hers, but again she held tightly to it.

He looked down and said, "You know so much, Claire. What's this supposed to mean?"

"What do you want it to mean?"

"I don't know."

"Well, you'd better try to figure it out."

"You are very smart, you know. You're also very dramatic."

"I'm a woman."

Jamal suddenly remembered something long buried. "But it's not just women," he said. "You know what my mother used to tell my dad when he showed out? She'd point to the door and say, 'Take the drama to your mama.'"

Claire smiled. "And that's what he did, isn't it? He took it somewhere else."

Jamal's face tightened. "Yeah, he left. One day he was gone. End of story."

"You loved him, didn't you?"

Jamal stared straight ahead. "I don't know."

"Well," she said, "maybe that's another thing you have to figure out."

A lanky boy with long black hair that constantly fell into his eyes and which he constantly rearranged with a shake of his head, stood at the podium reciting shakily: "The winter's darkness and cold is but a momentary prelude to the new day of spring. For while its grip seems endless, our perseverance is equal. Awaiting that moment of hope, new hope, that is home to our dreams." The young man glanced out at the auditorium nervously, shaking hair out of his eyes; he was aware that the audience was not certain he was done. "Thank you," he said with a frightened grin.

A scattering of polite applause rippled through the room. The student rushed off the stage and handed his paper to the elderly woman who was sitting next to Professor Crawford at a long table with ten other panelists composed of teachers and alumni. She dutifully inserted his paper in a thick file as Crawford moved to the podium.

"Thank you, Mr. Reilly," he said. "We still have quite a few more presentations, so if we could keep this break to five minutes."

Several of the students made for the exits. Crawford's eyes swept the room, and when they met Jamal's briefly they were full of cold contempt.

Claire, who noticed the look, said, "You have an enemy. Crawford."

"Yeah."

"You okay?"

"I don't know why I'm here. This isn't my scene."

"You want to leave?"

"I'll hang for a while."

"Crawford sent his report to the board last night—imagine, on a Sunday night! They're not wasting any time. Do you still need to be at that meeting?"

"That's what Bradley and my mom are talkin' about right now."

She nudged Jamal and said, "You want your hand back?"

He grinned. "It gets to be a habit."

"Jamal . . ." Claire half stood as she stared at the aisle.

Beard neatly trimmed, wearing a black turtleneck sweater and his tweed jacket, Forrester was plunging down the aisle, headed for the stage. He was looking down as he walked, and students, returning from the break, made way for him.

Crawford stood at the podium with his mouth open as he followed Forrester's progress toward the stage. A ripple started in the auditorium and began to gather momentum and force as word passed that the great William Forrester— more of a myth to many of them than a living, breathing reality—was . . . *here . . . in this auditorium.*

He reached the stairs leading to the stage and climbed them slowly. He pulled out his glasses and removed a sheet of paper from his jacket pocket, the microphone picking up the crackling sound of the paper as he smoothed it with his hands.

Everyone took a seat. The room was eerily quiet.

In a shaky voice, he said, "My name is William Forrester." He turned to glance at the photographs on the wall above and pointed to the one of himself. "I'm that one," he said.

A murmur arose from the room. Claire, stunned, turned to look at Jamal, but his focus was squarely on Forrester.

The old writer peered out at the packed room, and then at the table. "Professor Crawford?"

Crawford quickly rose to his feet. "Mr. Forrester . . ."

"I thought I might read a few remarks, if it's not an imposition."

"Certainly," said Crawford. "Whatever you might wish to share with us would be our privilege. I, personally, am . . . pleased . . . pleased and awed by your presence here." There was an underlying question in his words (why, exactly, *are* you here?) mixed in with the professor's unctuousness.

Forrester began to cough and couldn't stop. The elderly woman at the table, who was collecting students' papers, rushed to him with a glass of water.

He bowed his head toward her and smiled. "Thank you, madam," he said, and took a small sip.

He spread his hand over the paper and began to read. "Losing family," he said, "forces us to find our family. Not always the family that is our blood, but the family that will become our blood. Even that sense of family that is within ourselves."

There was not a sound in the room. The back doors began to crowd with teachers and other faculty.

"Life," he said, "is how you anticipate it. If we could look back on our lives, we would see that the most important events of our lives pass us by without our even knowing until years later how important they were. Sometimes we never know. Anticipation . . . We lose our own life's moments trying to find the ones that others tell us are important. And we end our lives with the question, How will I be remembered by others? Never thinking how we would remember ourselves."

Jamal squeezed Claire's hand until it hurt, but rather than pull away she squeezed back even harder. Their eyes were riveted on the stage.

"If life is indeed a game," he said, "we learn too late that it's a game that isn't won or lost. It's a game that too often simply isn't played. We search for answers, while never caring about the questions." Forrester coughed and drank more water. The shakiness was beginning to fade from his voice.

"And near the end . . . near the end . . . the only thing left to say is . . . I wish I had seen this, or I wish I had done that. But a

182

wish is only a hope that cannot be granted. We end our lives on a wish that can only be handed on to another who will desire the same. Anticipation."

The audience, completely still, caught up in the moment, watched as Forrester folded the paper, leaving it on the podium.

"I have never been much of a religious man," he said, "so if confession is good for the soul . . . well, I'm about to find out. As some of you may know, I have a reputation for having lived a solitary life." He took a deep breath before continuing. "Most of you are too young to even know what your wishes will be yet. But I look at the words that read, 'and near the end the wish is only a hope that cannot be granted.'" Forresters' breathing quickened and his lower lip began to tremble visibly. He held on to the podium with both hands. "And I realize that the one wish that was granted me so late in life . . . is one of friendship. May you have the fortune of building your hopes and your wishes on friendships that are strong." He nodded and said, "Thank you for your time."

The room responded with steady, polite applause. Crawford jumped to his feet, joining in acknowledging the legendary author. After the applause died down, he said, "Mr. Forrester, I'm sure I speak on behalf of everyone here at Mailor-Callow in thanking you for this very unexpected visit. The quality of your words . . . well, it's something everyone in this room should aspire to reach."

Crawford clapped his hands again and the rest of the room joined in.

"Mr. Forrester," he said with a warm smile, "if I might ask. . . to what do we owe this honor?"

The room grew quiet again, waiting for Forrester to respond. The old writer hesitated, then said, "There are a couple of reasons." He moved once again to the podium. "If you don't mind my taking a bit more of your time."

"Please," said Crawford, "by all means."

Claire leaned close to Jamal and whispered in his ear, "Do you have any idea what's going on?"

He nodded, not taking his eyes off Forrester. "Yeah."

As Crawford returned to the table, Forrester again faced the audience. "The reason I decided to speak on this stage today is because a good friend of mine wasn't allowed to. Most of you, I'm sure, benefit a great deal from the teaching you receive . . . a point I'm sure your teachers take great pains in impressing on you."

A wave of laughter spread through the auditorium.

Forrester waited through the laughter. "But there are a handful of writers who are blessed with the gift of putting words together, and when they choose to do so, we are given the choice of celebrating those words . . . or questioning where they came from." Forrester now looked directly at Professor Crawford. "You, sir, and your school chose to question the words of Mr. Jamal Wallace."

There was a loud buzz in the room at the mention of Jamal's name.

"I knew it, I *knew* it," Claire whispered. Jamal put a finger to his lips.

"Not only did your school question his words, it questioned far more. It questioned his integrity, of which there is a great deal, by making him write those words under the watchful eye of his own teachers—teachers who refused to believe that a young man of his background could possibly write the way he does."

Crawford gripped the edge of the table. He was no longer smiling.

"And how did your board of trustees respond? By allowing that humiliation to happen in exchange for a meaningless game of basketball. That is how *your* institution responded."

Crawford rose from the table, raising his arm in a halting gesture, but Forrester froze him with a glare.

"A final comment, please." Again Forrester had to gather himself to contain his emotion; his voice was trembling as he said, "What no one was willing to see—what no one even *thought* to see—and I include myself . . . was a young man willing to walk out on a game that meant everything to him . . . because . . . this is difficult . . . I'm sorry . . . because he had the simple honor to protect someone who was willing to walk out on him. That's the quality of this young man all of you would have seen had you merely looked. Or taken time to listen to him."

With a shaking hand, Forrester lifted the glass of water to his lips. He then removed his glasses and wiped his eyes. There wasn't a sound in the room.

He continued, finally saying, "Show this student of yours, this talented and fine young man, a mere fraction of the loyalty he's proven he deserves." Forrester began to back away from the podium. "And to those students who *will* be given the chance to share their words, my apologies for taking your time."

As he walked off the stage the applause began, at first slowly, scattered throughout the room, but then growing louder with every step the old writer took, until it reached a peak of foot stomping and whistling.

Crawford pounded his gavel on the table.

"Mr. Forrester," he said as the noise began to abate, "while we do appreciate the opportunity to have you visit our school, we do *not* appreciate those unfamiliar with the rules of the school imposing their own judgment."

Forrester, who had left the stage, turned back to the professor. "Mr. Crawford, *I* was the one who allowed Mr. Wallace to use that essay, which he has managed brilliantly to make his own— and if it's not plagiarism in my eyes, it cannot be in yours."

Crawford fumbled for words. "I don't understand. It seems to me there's some confusion—"

"Oh, and one more thing. The words I read today? I only read them. They were written by Jamal Wallace."

Crawford stared at Forrester in astonishment. "I don't understand," he said again.

The elderly woman with the box of competition entries rose from the table and walked to the podium, her footsteps resounding throughout an auditorium struck dumb by the unfolding events. She carried the file holding the other entries. She slipped on her glasses, picked up a paper and spoke into the microphone.

"Mr. Wallace—would you stand, please?"

Jamal disengaged his hand from Claire's and slowly got to his feet.

"This paper of yours has been returned to the competition, as of now."

"Thank you."

She then turned to Forrester and said, "As senior faculty member of this school, I think I can speak for the others when I offer you our sincerest gratitude for what you've done today. You have righted a grave injustice." She turned back to Jamal and smiled. "Mr. Wallace, as chair of the faculty board, I excuse you so that you can show Mr. Forrester out . . . and you are most certainly excused from next week's board meeting."

As she stuck Jamal's paper inside a file, there was a thunderous ovation from the students. John Coleridge stood on his chair and yelled out, "Go, Jamal. Go, man!"

Jamal quickly ushered Forrester out to the street. The old man was exhausted and leaned against Jamal as they walked to Eighty-sixth Street.

"We have your brother to thank," Forrester said after a moment's silence.

"Yeah. He came through for me. I guess for both of us."

"For both of us, Jamal. It took your words to wake me up."

"You know something? I had a feeling you would come."

"You did?"

"I sat there in the auditorium . . . this is strange to say, but I sensed your presence."

They walked in silence for a moment and then Forrester said, "So . . . I guess the decisions are yours to make once again."

"I'm guessing you're gonna say something like . . . they always were."

Forrester shook his head. "No more lessons."

They reached the subway stop at Eighty-sixth Street and Lexington.

"Don't tell me you're gonna take a train, William."

Forrester smiled. "Apparently I'm growing braver in my old age. Thanks in large measure to you."

Jamal regarded his friend with affection. "Maybe we've learned from each other."

"That's usually the way it is between friends."

"So what happens now?"

"For you?"

"No. For you."

"Well, my guess is that today's little public appearance will spark new interest in my work. So it might be the right moment to take some time away."

"Yeah? Where?"

"I have this native land that I haven't seen for years."

"Ireland?"

Forrester said with a trace of impatience, "Scotland, for goodness sake!"

"William," Jamal said with a grin, "I was just kidding, okay?"

Forrester scowled, then broke out in a grin. "My student," he said. "My friend. Always one step ahead of me."

"Be sure to write," Jamal said.

"You, too."

There was no hug, no handshake, only a look of love between the old man and the boy. Then Forrester turned and walked down the steps to the subway. Jamal watched him go and slowly raised his hand in a last salute.

Epilogue

A year passed. Jamal was now a senior at Mailor-Callow and exuding a confidence that would have seemed impossible six months earlier. After countless nights of discussion and hundreds of phone calls and e-mails, he and Claire had solemnly pledged themselves as boyfriend and girlfriend. He was once again hanging out with his old friends, having set up a once-a-week tutoring program involving Fly, Damon and Kenzo. They read books together and handed in writing assignments. At first they had balked at Jamal's plan, but all three were making real progress, Fly showing a marked talent for ribald humor.

One Monday morning in the early spring, Jamal arrived at his locker and absently popped it open with the flat of his hand, using the Claire method. There were letters taped inside, all of them written on thin international airmail paper, all from Forrester.

John Coleridge, whose locker was next to Jamal's, said, "You heard from William lately?"

"Got a letter last week. He's checkin' up on these college recruiters."

Coleridge grinned. "He thinks he's your father, Jamal."

"I know."

"I was just down in the office. There's another guy asking for you. They'll probably pull you out of homeroom."

"Oh yeah? I didn't expect anybody today."

"I hope it's Princeton. It would be great to be together, man."

"I'd better check it out," Jamal said.

The office was busy as he entered, but a middle-aged man in a dark pinstripe suit spotted him right away.

"Jamal?"

"Yeah."

"I'm Steve Sanderson. Would you please join me in here?" He indicated one of the small conference rooms off the main room.

The man held the door open for him. Jamal walked inside and slumped into a chair, opening his notebook as he prepared for another pitch.

Sanderson closed the door and sat at a small round table, waving to Jamal to take a seat beside him. He was carrying a small wooden box and a briefcase. He opened the briefcase and regarded Jamal seriously.

"I've heard a lot about you," he said. He smiled briefly. "All good things."

"Thank you," Jamal said. "What college are you from? I should warn you that I'm already seriously considering about six schools."

Sanderson listened patiently. When Jamal was finished, he said, "I'm with the law offices of Roberts and Carter, here in Manhattan. We serve as legal representatives for William Forrester."

"William? But . . . why are you here?"

"Jamal, we've received word that William has passed away."

"He died?" Jamal stared at the lawyer. "William's dead?"

"We felt it best to tell you as soon as possible, rather than your finding out from television or the newspapers."

"When did he die?"

"Last night. He died peacefully in his sleep."

"But what did he die of? He wrote me last week and he didn't say anything was wrong. He sounded just fine."

"William had cancer, Jamal. The doctors found it almost two years ago."

Jamal shielded his eyes with a hand and stared at the desk. "I didn't even know him two years ago. He never said anything."

Sanderson let a moment pass before saying, "He left very specific instructions concerning his estate. He took care of these matters months ago. In closing up his apartment, which will be done this week, there are a number of items he has willed to you—rather large items—which we can put in storage until you decide what to do with them." He put on his glasses and read from a list: "An antique cherry wood desk. A telescope. An Underwood manual typewriter. A pair of binoculars. A black leather recliner." Sanderson reached down and handed Jamal the wooden box and a key. Taped to the top of the box was an envelope. "This he instructed us to get to you as soon as possible."

Jamal looked at the lawyer and said, "I had so many things I still wanted to tell him."

*

That afternoon, Jamal opened the door to Forrester's apartment and led his mother and Terrell inside. He was carrying the box that Sanderson had given him. Mrs. Wallace looked around the living room in wonder.

"It's hard to believe something like this . . . this grand . . . exists in our neighborhood."

"I felt the same way when I first saw it," Jamal said in a whisper. Flooded with memories, he was trying to control his emotions as he studied the familiar books and furniture.

"He must have been quite a man."

"You're right, Ma. He was."

Jamal walked over to Forrester's desk and glided his hand over the old Underwood typewriter. He lightly pulled the carriage return.

"William would work at this typewriter," he said. "I'd be right next to him, workin' away at the other one." He shook his head, fighting against the enormous pull of the past.

He turned to the window—the window where it all began for him—and took a few steps forward. He saw that it was

190

dirty. He wiped away the dust with his shirtsleeve and opened the window a crack. Staring across the street, toward Richmond High and the basketball court, he spotted a flash of red—a scarlet tanager. He listened to its soft springtime call and watched it hop from limb to limb. He remembered the other scarlet tanager, the one William had videotaped with such excitement in what seemed like a world ago. He squeezed his eyes tight to hold back the tears.

He sat on a bench beside the basketball court, waiting for Fly. The box was on the ground at his feet. He removed the letter that was taped to the box and carefully opened it. He had been holding off this moment since the lawyer had given him the box that morning, but he could wait no longer. As he began to read, a tear streaked down his face. He quickly wiped it away.

Dear Jamal (the letter began),

Someone I once knew wrote that all we need do is accept the wishes and the hopes and the dreams. You need to know that while I knew so very early that you would realize your dreams, I never imagined I would once again realize my own.

Seasons change, young man. And while I may have waited until the winter of my life to see the things I've seen this past year, there is no doubt I would have waited too long had it not been for you.

Take what is in this box. It is for you, and it is to you. Take it and give it to the world as you see fit. Any explanations and interpretations should come from you in a prefatory note of some kind.

Goodbye, Jamal. I can rest now, assured that you will carry on.

Jamal's eyes were moist and glowed with excitement as he opened the box and studied the top page of a thick manuscript.
Sunset. A novel by William Forrester.

Foreword to be written by Jamal Wallace.

"Hey," said a voice behind him.

He knew it was Fly, but for a moment he didn't turn, not wanting his friend to see his tears.

"You gonna be around a while?" Fly said.

Jamal tucked the letter in the box and closed it. He grabbed the ball at his side as he pulled himself up. "Yeah—I'm gonna be around."

He tossed the ball to Fly, still embarrassed to look his way.

The two friends walked onto the court.

Fly looked at him out of the corner of his eye. "You okay, man?"

"Never better," Jamal answered. "Toss me the ball. I got a new move for you."

He double clutched, slithered free of Fly and rattled the rim with a happy scream.

"Yeah," said Fly, "all *right*. Looks like the man is back!"